She kissed him

"It's complicated."

She pulled her head back and stared into his light brown eyes. After a year and twenty-one days, after letting her think he was dead, he needed a much better explanation. "Tell me about it."

She wasn't letting him run away after giving her a whisper of sweet talk and "it's complicated." She needed a hell of a lot more than that. She slid down his body and planted her boots on the ground. "Sit down, Wade."

"I already told you. I can't—"

"We can do this the easy way or the hard way."

He frowned. "What?"

The hard way, it was. She stalked around him until she had the uphill position. From there, it was easy to shove his shoulder and hook his legs out from under him. As soon as his butt hit the dirt, she was on him. After taking away his rifle, she flipped him onto his belly and cuffed his hands behind his back.

"Wade Calloway, you're under arrest."

COLORADO WILDFIRE

USA TODAY Bestselling Author

CASSIE MILES

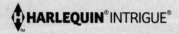

To the most excellent uncles, Charlie and C.J. Climp.
And, as always, to Rick.

Recycling programs
for this product may
not exist in your area.

ISBN-13: 978-0-373-69888-2

Colorado Wildfire

Printed in U.S.A.

Cassie Miles, a *USA TODAY* bestselling author, lives in Colorado. After raising two daughters and cooking tons of macaroni and cheese for her family, Cassie is trying to be more adventurous in her culinary efforts. She's discovered that almost anything tastes better with wine. When she's not plotting Harlequin Intrigue books, Cassie likes to hang out at the Denver Botanical Gardens near her high-rise home.

Books by Cassie Miles

Harlequin Intrigue

Mountain Midwife
Sovereign Sheriff
Baby Battalion
Unforgettable
Midwife Cover
Mommy Midwife
Montana Midwife
Hostage Midwife
Mountain Heiress
Snowed In
Snow Blind
Mountain Retreat
Colorado Wildfire

Visit the Author Profile page at
Harlequin.com for more titles.

CAST OF CHARACTERS

Samantha "Sam" Calloway—The newly elected sheriff of Swain County took over the job when her husband died a year ago.

Wade Calloway—The former sheriff was forced to fake his own death to protect his wife and daughter.

Jennifer Calloway—The five-year-old daughter of Sam and Wade.

Caleb Schmidt—A Swain County deputy who has been on the job for nearly thirty years.

Pansy Gardener—One of the 911 dispatchers who sometimes babysits for Jennifer.

Ty Baxter—An FBI special agent based in Denver who grew up on the family ranch in Swain County.

Logan Baxter—Ty's brother, who runs the ranch.

Everett Hurtado—The FBI supervisory special agent, Ty's boss, coordinates the investigation of smuggling in Swain County.

Justin Hobbs—The fire marshal has his hands full with a wildfire approaching the only town in the county.

Trevor Natchez—A lieutenant with the Colorado State Patrol, he does everything by the book.

Drew Morrissey—The state patrolman is the first victim.

William Crowe—The corrupt undercover DEA agent is in prison.

El Jefe—Also in prison, he's a high-ranking member of the Esteban Cartel.

Tony Reyes—Under orders from the cartel, he led the assault on Sam and Wade.

Dana Gregg and Lyle McFee—Both were assassinated in the first crime.

Chapter One

Sheriff Samantha Calloway hadn't cried this much since her husband went missing and was presumed dead. She swabbed the moisture from her cheeks with the back of her hand. These tears didn't come from sorrow. Smoke had got into her eyes.

She parked her white SUV with the sheriff's logo at a deserted intersection, climbed out and rested her elbows on the front fender to steady her binoculars. Beyond a wide field that was green with the new growth of early spring, she could see the approaching wildfire.

Though the crimson flames were far away, barely visible behind a distant ridge, smoke consumed the landscape. A stinging haze draped the spires of pine and spruce at the edge of Swain County in the high Rocky Mountains.

When she licked her lips, she tasted ash on her tongue. Her pale blue eyes continued to ooze with tears.

Caleb Schmidt, a deputy who had been with the sheriff's department for thirty years, one year longer than Sam had been alive, had followed her to this location. He got out of his vehicle and strutted toward her. A short, wiry man, Caleb thrust out his chest and swung his arms when he walked. Maybe he thought the posture made him look bigger. He pulled the dark blue bandana down from his mouth and squinted at her through his thick glasses.

"It's time," he said in a voice of doom, "time to start emergency evacuation procedures."

"Not yet."

"Doggone it, Sheriff, we gotta hustle and—"

"I've been in contact with the proper officials," she interrupted. "Fire Marshal Hobbs will tell me in plenty of time if we need to evacuate."

Caleb scoffed. Before he could say anything more, she stretched out her long arm and tugged on his bandana. "Where's your smoke mask?"

"Where's yours?" he retorted.

This morning when she'd started out, she had two boxes full of disposable ventilator masks that she'd gone to the trouble of ordering even though they weren't in her meager budget. Before noon, she'd given them all away without saving one for herself. Her late husband, Wade, would have pointed to her behavior as an example of her too-too-responsible attitude. And, she admitted to herself, Wade would have been right. Sam knew she couldn't take care of others if she didn't take care of herself first, but the other way around felt more natural.

"The wind's picking up," Caleb muttered. "The fire's on the move. I hear it's already burned two thousand acres. I'm advising you to reconsider."

"If I had reason to believe it might reach town, I wouldn't hesitate to get everybody out." Her five-year-old daughter was smack-dab in the middle of Woodridge at the sheriff's office in the two-story, red stone Swain County Courthouse, where the dispatch/911 operators were keeping an eye on her. Sam's regular babysitter had an asthmatic toddler and had driven down to Denver to get away from this awful smoke.

"We gotta be smart, gotta move fast." Caleb would not give up; he was a feisty little pug with a bone. "It ain't going to be easy to get some of these old coots to leave their houses."

He was right about that. A mandated evacuation of Woodridge would be a nightmare. Her county was the smallest in the state in terms of acreage and population. They didn't have a ski resort or a condo development or fertile land for farming. The entire sheriff's department consisted of twelve people, including Sam.

She swabbed the moisture from under her eyes and stared at her deputy. "I'm not going to change my mind. No mandatory evacuation unless the fire marshal says there's an imminent threat. Is that clear?"

Grudgingly, he said, "I guess you're the boss."

You got that right. None of her six deputies had been thrilled when she took over her husband's job as sheriff. That was over a year ago, and she'd been duly elected last February for one big fat obvious reason: she was the best qualified. As a teenager, she'd done volunteer search and rescue. She'd been top of her class at the police academy. Not to mention her three years' experience as a cop in Grand Junction before she married Wade. Still, her deputies second-guessed her at every turn.

"Deputy Schmidt, I want you to stay right here and keep an eye on things. That's an order."

"Yes, ma'am," he said, properly chastised.

The two-lane asphalt road pointed south was one of the few direct routes toward the flames. "Except for firefighting personnel, no vehicles are allowed to pass."

"And what are you going to do?"

She spotted the black Range Rover she'd been waiting for. "I need to go with Ty Baxter to check on a property."

"It's that FBI safe house. Am I right?"

"You know I can't tell you." Not that the location was a well-kept secret. "And you're not supposed to say anything about the safe house, either."

He mimed zipping his lips, fastening a lock and throwing away the key. Then he pulled up his bandana to cover his mouth and marched toward his vehicle.

FBI special agent Ty Baxter jumped from his Rover and came toward her with long strides. In his Stetson, denim jeans, snakeskin boots and white shirt with a yoke and pearly snaps, he could have looked as phony as a drugstore cowboy. But Ty pulled it off. After all, he was the real deal, the son of a local rancher.

He'd been her husband's best friend. They'd gone to school together, played football together and dated the same girls. Ty had won the heart of the prom queen. The whole county had been heartbroken when he and Loretta moved to Denver to pursue his career.

He gave her a big hug. "Looking good, Sam."

"Liar."

She knew better. Her blue eyes were bloodshot. Instead of makeup, she had jagged smears of ash across her face. Under her beige cowboy hat, her long brown hair was pulled back in a tight braid that hung halfway down to her waist. Her boxy khaki uniform wasn't designed to flatter. Not to mention the heavy-duty bulletproof vest under her shirt and the utility belt that circled her waist. On top of all that, she was fairly sure that she had pit stains.

"How's Jenny?" he asked.

"Getting taller every day."

"Like you."

Sam was six feet tall in her boots. "I kind of hoped she wouldn't inherit the giraffe gene."

Ty grinned and his dark brown eyes twinkled. "Both her parents are giraffes."

Wade had been six feet five inches tall. Whenever Sam was with Ty, her thoughts drifted toward her husband. The two men had been close. They even looked kind of alike. Both were tall and lean. Both had brown eyes and dark hair. Ty had been with Wade when he died.

She shook off the memories and returned Ty's easygoing smile. "You got here from Denver really fast."

"I was already on my way when I called about the safe house. Sam, there's something important I need to tell you."

She nodded. "We can talk on the way. We'll take my SUV. I need to be able to hear my dispatcher."

After reminding Deputy Schmidt to keep this route blocked, she got behind the steering wheel. When Ty joined her, he was carrying a gym bag from his Rover. Before he buckled up, he reached inside and took out his smooth, black, lethal-looking Beretta 9 mm semiautomatic pistol.

"Whoa," she said. "Are you planning to shoot the fire?"

"I like to be prepared." He clipped the holster to his belt. "Don't you?"

Prepared for what? Sam was wary. First, Ty had mentioned "something important" he wanted to talk about. Now he was packing a gun. She had a bad feeling about what fresh disaster might be lurking around the next corner. Hoping to avoid bigger problems, she asked about his family. "Are your twins still playing T-ball?"

"They're getting pretty good," he said, "and Loretta signed on to be coach of their team."

"Good for her." Sheriff Sam was happy to support women who broke the stereotypes.

"Surprised the hell out of me. I never thought my Loretta was athletic, but she's getting into sports."

"Imagine that."

Apparently, Ty had forgotten that Loretta was a rodeo barrel racer and a black-diamond skier. Because his little Loretta was capable of looking like a princess, he forgot her kick-ass side. Wade had never made that mistake with Samantha.

The first three miles of paved road swept across an open field. Under the smoky haze, the tall prairie grasses mingled with bright splashes of scarlet and blue wildflowers. Then the road turned to graded gravel, still two lanes but bumpy. The scenery closed in around them as they entered a narrow canyon.

While she guided the SUV through a series of turns that followed the winding path of Horny Toad Creek, they chatted about family and how much Ty and Loretta missed living in the mountains. His dad wanted him to move back to Swain County and help out at the ranch.

"That would mean giving up your career," Sam said. "There's not much need for an FBI special agent around here."

He exhaled a sigh. "You and Wade had the right idea. Decide where you want to live, and then find a way to make a living."

When she and her husband started out, she hadn't been so sure they'd made a good decision. They were newlyweds with six acres and a good well outside Wood-ridge. She'd just quit her cop job and was trying to make ends meet on one salary. Within two months, she was pregnant. While expecting and unemployed, she was able to oversee every step of the construction.

The house they built was perfectly tailored for them. She'd even made the kitchen counters a few inches taller so she didn't have to stoop when she was chopping to-matillos for green salsa. She and Wade had made love in every room and on the deck and in the garage…

"The turn is coming up," Ty said as he squinted to-ward the left side of the road.

"I know where it is." She checked on the safe house whenever she was in the area. It hadn't been occupied in months.

He took a water bottle from his gym bag, unscrewed the lid and poured a splash over a red bandana. Like Caleb, he tied the bandana across the lower half of his face.

She couldn't stop herself from being Miss Know-It-All. "The fire marshal says the weave of a cotton bandana isn't fine enough to prevent ash particles from getting through."

"Don't care," he said. "The wetness makes breath-ing easier. Here's the turnoff."

After a quick left, she drove on a one-lane road that ascended a rugged slope. The safe house clung to the side of a granite cliff and faced away from the road. If she hadn't known where she was going, Sam would never have found this place amid the rocks and trees.

When she exited her vehicle, the smoke swirled around her ankles in a thick miasma. From the wraparound porch of the house, she and Ty had a clear view of the wildfire.

The blaze danced across the upper edge of a hogback ridge. With the sun going down, the billowing clouds of smoke turned an angry red. It looked like the gates of hell. A chopper flew over the leaping flames and dropped a load of retardant on the forest.

She watched as Ty wandered around to the side of the house toward the long attached garage. "Looking for something?"

"I'm being thorough."

She noticed his hand resting on his belt near his holster, ready to make a quick draw. What was making him so suspicious? "Is there something I should know about?"

He joined her on the porch. "Long as I'm here, I might as well look around inside."

His fingers hovered over a keypad outside the front door. He glanced over his shoulder at her. "Do you happen to…?"

"Remember the code to deactivate the alarm?" She grinned and rattled off six digits. The Swain County sheriff always had the code. When the alarm went off, it rang through to her office, and she had to come up here to turn it off.

Before she could follow Ty inside, her cell phone rang. It was the fire marshal—a call she needed to take. As she answered, she signaled to Ty to go ahead without her.

"Marshal Hobbs," she said, "what can you tell me?"

"The fire is mostly contained." His voice was raspy. Sore throats must be an occupational hazard. "You won't need to evacuate the town, especially not if it rains tonight like it's supposed to."

"That's the good news," she said. "What's the bad?"

"Well, Sheriff, I've got a favor to ask. The chopper

pilot spotted three hikers on the road by Horny Toad Creek. I can't spare the men to pick them up. Could you take care of it?"

"No problem," she assured him. "I happen to be in that area right now. How do you know they're hikers?"

"The pilot said they were wearing backpacks. You know the look."

"I sure do. Keep me posted on the fire."

When Ty came out of the safe house, she waved him over to her SUV and told him about the hikers who needed a pickup. "I can't imagine any sensible reason they'd hike near a wildfire. These guys must be thrill-seekers or morons."

"Or reporters," Ty said.

"Same thing."

She'd had her fill of reporters after Wade's death. They wouldn't leave her alone, constantly pestered her for interviews or photos of her and Jenny. All she ever wanted was to grieve in private. But Wade's accident was news.

One year and twenty-one days ago, he'd gone bow hunting with Ty and two other feds, including Ty's boss, Everett Hurtado. A kayaker on the river had lost control in the rapids, and Wade had jumped into the frigid waters to rescue him. The kayaker had survived. Wade had been swept away by the white water. His body had never been found.

As Sam started the engine in her SUV, dark thoughts gnawed at the edge of her mind. She had plenty of things to worry about: the fire, the hikers, the lack of ventilation masks and Ty's "important" news. But she could never escape the pain and the sorrow that had taken up permanent residence inside her. She'd never forget the loss of her husband. He was her soul mate, her dearest lover and best friend.

As she drove along the road that followed the twists and turns of the creek, she turned her head toward Ty. *Might as well get this over with.* "What's this important thing you want to tell me?"

"You know, Sam, I can hardly look at you without thinking of Wade."

"Back at you, Ty. You were one of his best friends. You grew up together." She guided the SUV into a more open area that deviated from the path of the creek. "Is this important message about Wade?"

"How do you feel about him? Are you, maybe, looking at other men?"

"Hell no." There was no other man, and there never would be. She only had room in her heart for Jenny and for Wade.

The road straightened out. The right side was a field behind a barbed-wire fence. To the left, a gently rising hillside climbed into a thick, old growth forest. If the fire got this far, these hills would go up like dry tinder.

Ty cleared his throat. "I was just thinking…"

"If you're going to say that it's time to move on, that I should get out there in the world and start dating, forget it. Don't you dare tell me how to grieve."

He pointed across the windshield to the left side of the road. "Over there."

In the shadow of a tall cottonwood, she spotted a dark green sedan that apparently had gone across the shoulder and run into the shrubs, rocks and trees at the side of the road. She parked behind it. "Maybe our three hikers came from that car."

"Makes sense," Ty said. "Maybe they had an accident and are trying to walk back to civilization. But why didn't we see them on the road? Why would they go toward the fire?"

She left the SUV and went to investigate. The green sedan blended into the trees and shrubs, which was why the helicopter pilot hadn't noticed it. She saw the outline of a man's head and shoulders behind the steering wheel.

He wasn't moving.

Chapter Two

A rising sense of dread crept up her spine and raised the fine hairs on the nape of her neck. Unlike the distant threat of the raging wildfire, this trouble was only a few steps away. Sam adjusted the holster on her belt for easier access to the Glock 23 she'd used to win marksmanship contests at the academy. Never once had she fired her pistol on the job: her stun gun was usually enough. But her cop instincts told her that this situation might require more firepower.

"Sir," she called out as she moved closer to the vehicle, "I'm with the sheriff's department. Show me your hands. Sir?"

Ty came up beside her. He held his Beretta at the ready. "I suggest we proceed with caution."

"Ya think?"

He immediately backed off. "I'm following your lead, Sam."

Even if Swain County wasn't a hotbed of criminal activity, she knew the standard procedures and would adhere to them as much as possible. She pulled her pistol from the holster and went to the driver's side. The window was down. Fully expecting to find the driver sleeping or drunk, she angled around until she could see inside.

"Sir, are you…?" The words froze in her mouth.

He'd been shot in the chest. The front of his plaid flannel shirt was drenched in blood from his neck to his gut. *Oh God, what do I do next? What's the procedure?* She should check for a pulse, assess his condition. But she didn't need to touch his pale jowls to know the flesh would be cold. His sightless eyes stared directly at her.

"He's dead," Ty said.

"Yes." She could barely speak. Her throat was dry.

"We need to be careful. The killer might still be nearby."

Gathering her courage, she backed away from the sedan and scanned the area, peering through the smoke at the rocks, shrubs and trees. No one else was in sight, but these hills were full of hiding places. A murderer wouldn't put up a billboard to announce his presence.

But would he run away? Was he waiting for them? Harsh little flashes of tension and fear made it impossible for her to concentrate. *Oh, Wade, I miss you.* He would have known what to do. He was a born leader; giving orders came easily to him. Somehow, she had to pull herself together.

She cleared her throat. "We have to find the hikers."

"Do you think they did this?"

"I don't know."

But she didn't think those three men with backpacks were in this area by coincidence. Either they were friends of the deceased who were on the run or they were killers.

Ty gently touched her shoulder. "Are you all right?"

"This is my first murder case."

"I'm here to help."

She'd seen dead bodies before, usually people who passed away from old age or due to an accident. And she'd arrested plenty of bad guys who had hurt someone else. The local violence had always stopped far short of murder.

"I can do this," she said.

"Hell yes."

She slapped her Glock back into the holster. "I want this investigation to be done right." She took out a pair of baby blue latex gloves and slipped them on.

"Do you always have gloves in your pocket?"

"Not my pocket. My utility belt." She passed a pair to him. "I keep them in here."

"Isn't that the place where you should be packing a second magazine for your Glock?"

"Here's the thing, Ty. I've never fired all thirteen rounds from this gun. I'll carry one mag of extra bullets, but the second one is overkill. But I've found the gloves come in handy. I am a mom, after all."

"Uh-huh."

"Last time I used my latex gloves was at Jenny's kindergarten class when we were making a collage of forest animals."

He nodded slowly. "What's our next move?"

That was a good question. Swain County didn't have the facilities to deal with a murder. They had a small clinic and a dentist who doubled as county coroner but no hospital for an autopsy. For forensics, she used a fingerprint kit that she usually carried in her SUV. She had no access to DNA data analysis or a mass spectrometer or any other fancy tools.

In usual circumstances, she'd step aside and happily

turn this investigation over to the Colorado Bureau of Investigation or maybe the Grand Junction police. But today was different. Today, there was a wildfire that just might reach this car and obliterate the scene of the crime.

She took her cell phone from her pocket. "First, I'm going to take photos of the crime scene and dust for prints. Then you and me are going to load this body into the back of my SUV and cart him to the nearest hospital."

"Why move him?"

Pointing toward the flames, she said, "So the body won't be incinerated along with the rest of the evidence."

With her phone camera, she took a picture of the windshield and the front end of the car, which was crumpled against the trunk of the cottonwood. The damage wasn't severe, causing her to think the car hadn't been going very fast at the time of impact. Pleased with herself for drawing that conclusion, she made a complete circle around the sedan, taking pictures of the whole car. No skid marks in the gravel behind the car. The driver hadn't applied the brakes.

A theory began to form in her mind. The man behind the steering wheel was already dead when the car hit the tree. Her conclusion fit the evidence. Wade would have been proud of her. He'd always said that she was a natural-born cop, not surprising since her father was a captain in the Portland PD.

She returned to the front window and made observations, sticking her head inside. The dead man was covered in blood, but the rest of the front seat was fairly clean. She looked over her shoulder at Ty. "I don't think this sedan is our primary crime scene."

"What do you mean?"

"I think he was killed somewhere else and then put in the front seat, which is why there's no spatter. And he didn't crash this car. It was pushed off the road into the tree."

"How do you know that?"

After outlining her prior conclusions, she stepped away from the window so he could see the final bit of evidence for himself. "No keys in the ignition."

He peered inside, taking care not to get blood on his white shirt with the pearly snaps, and then he cursed. "I recognize this guy."

Had she heard him right? "You know him?"

"He's a cop." Ty pulled his head out of the car and stood up straight. "A state patrolman. I think his name is Morrissey. Wade introduced us."

Her husband had been well acquainted with all the law-enforcement guys who worked in and around Swain County. Like her own deputies, they hadn't been as friendly with Sam. "We'd better do everything right. The staties can be as annoying as you FBI guys. Lieutenant Natchez is a real pill."

"Agreed. I've met Natchez." Ty whipped out his cell phone. "Do you want me to contact him?"

"I guess that's the right thing to do."

If the situation had been reversed, and someone had found Deputy Caleb Schmidt's body, she'd want to be among the first who were informed. She wasn't looking forward to seeing Natchez. Somehow, he'd get everything turned around and make this murder her fault.

While Ty placed the call, she continued photographing

the inside of the vehicle, starting with the front driver's side and working her way around. No blood at all in the backseat. When she opened the passenger-side door, she saw a handgun. An attractive piece, it was a Colt revolver with an inlaid copper-colored design on the grip.

The weapon belonged to her husband.

WADE CALLOWAY EXERTED every bit of his willpower to keep himself from charging down the hill, grabbing his wife and planting a big, hard kiss on her soft, pink lips. The urge almost overwhelmed him. He couldn't stand to watch her anymore. Ducking down behind a tall boulder at the edge of the forest, he squeezed his eyelids shut, fighting his desperate need to be with Samantha, his angel.

Now wasn't the time or the place.

If he showed his face, she'd be in danger.

What the hell was she doing on this road? Why did she have to be the one who discovered the body? His fingers curled into a fist, and he hammered the ground beneath his boots. Life was not fair!

For more than a year, he'd fantasized about what it would be like when he came home to his sweet wife. She'd come running toward him with her long brown hair streaming behind her in a silky banner. Her clothing— always flimsy in his imagination—would outline her slender legs and supple torso. Her laughter would ring out, and their perfect daughter would join in with hugs and kisses. Jenny and Sam would treat him to a hero's welcome.

He peeked around the edge of the boulder. Samantha stalked around the vehicle. He couldn't actually see her scowl from this distance, but he could tell that she was frustrated and annoyed. More than annoyed—anger radiated from her in waves that were even hotter than the wildfire.

He had a real bad feeling that this hostile version of Samantha was the woman who would greet him when he stepped out of hiding. He could hope for her forgiveness but didn't expect it.

His life—which used to be so very fine—had become one snafu after another. The murder of Drew Morrissey was the latest blunder. Somebody should have been watching the bum, keeping him from getting shot. Not that Wade intended to waste any tears on Morrissey. The man was a traitor to his uniform. Protecting him would have been a smart strategy. Morrissey was cowardly and weak. He might have turned on his partners in crime. Most likely, that ratlike tendency to squeal was probably why the scumbag was dead.

Wade had found the body behind the steering wheel of his car about a half hour ago and had staked out the area, hoping that the killer or killers might come back. And if they did, what would he do? He wanted to take these guys into custody, to lock them up and throw away the keys. It wasn't that easy. He'd spent the past year in protective custody, waiting to testify and make things right.

Three days ago the legal case had collapsed for the umpteenth time, and Wade decided he wasn't willing to wait, especially not after he'd caught a glimpse of a man in the federal courthouse whom he vaguely remembered. The name hadn't come to him. But he'd seen this guy before. And that was enough of a threat to get him moving. If the bad guys had seen him and knew he was alive and waiting to testify, Samantha and Jenny would be in danger.

He'd escaped from his handlers in Texas and made his way back here. Last night, he'd slept in the FBI safe house, thankful they hadn't changed the security code from the time he was sheriff. From the house, he'd picked up some important supplies: two semiautomatic pistols and a hunting rifle. In the attached garage, he'd found a lightweight Honda motorcycle with heavy-tread tires that made it suitable for off-road or on-road driving.

He had intended to find Samantha and Jenny this morning, to take them away with him. A lot of people, including his supposed friend Ty, would tell him that he shouldn't return to Colorado. The whole reason they faked his death was so nobody would come after Samantha or Jenny to hurt him. But Wade couldn't stay away.

He'd find a way to keep his family safe. It might not be comfortable or pretty, but at least they'd be together. That was what he should have done in the first place. The time apart had been gut-wrenching.

He peeked out from behind the rock again. Damn, she was pretty. He wanted to caress every inch of Samantha's beautiful body, to smell the clean fragrance of her shampoo, to taste her mouth and stare into her cool blue eyes. Not even the boxy sheriff uniform could disguise her long legs and well-toned arms.

Not to brag, but he'd done some bodybuilding of his own. One of the ways he'd distracted himself for all these months was by working out. He'd tightened his six-pack, and the biceps and triceps in his arms were sharply defined. Would Samantha notice? He couldn't wait until she ran her long, slender fingers down his chest and commented on his new physical conditioning.

From the road, he heard her bark an order at Ty. "Just do what I say. Do it now."

Wade chuckled under his breath. "That's my sweet, delicate angel."

He craned his neck so he could see the road more clearly. She had the door of the sedan open and was messing around with the dead body. What the hell was she doing?

Chapter Three

She might not be an expert on how to process a crime scene, but Sam was in charge here. Ty needed to remember that little fact. Swain County was her jurisdiction. And she wanted to move the body of Colorado state patrolman Drew Morrissey into the rear of her SUV before this scene was engulfed in flames and all the evidence destroyed.

"Come on, Ty, let's do it."

He groaned. "Didn't your friend the fire marshal tell you that the burn wouldn't get this far?"

"Marshal Hobbs said the town would be safe. This location is miles and miles away from there." She slapped her hands together to start the action. "You take his head, and I'll take his legs."

Ty slipped into his black FBI windbreaker to protect his white shirt, but he still complained. "Why do I get the messy end of the body?"

"Don't be such a wuss. You're stronger than me and the top half of the body is heavier."

Also, she intended to use the few minutes when she was alone by Morrissey's car to shove Wade's copper-handled revolver under the seat. Removing evidence would be wrong. She was certain about that. Hiding the evidence might be kind of, maybe, a little bit acceptable. *It's not. I know better.*

But she needed a couple more minutes to figure out what to do about a gun that should have been locked in a case at her house. *It could be the murder weapon.* Maybe she'd tell Ty about it before Morrissey's supervisor got here. She definitely didn't want Lieutenant Natchez to use her husband's fancy revolver to tie her to a murder scene.

When Ty pulled Morrissey away from the seat, the man's head flopped forward against the steering wheel. Seeing him was different than touching. The stench of death cut through the smoke as she helped Ty manipulate the dead weight. Morrissey's arms dangled. His legs were as floppy as a rag doll. There wasn't anything she could do about the revolver until Ty had the body halfway out of the seat.

In a quick move, she ducked inside the car, shoved the weapon under the passenger's seat, emerged and slammed the driver's-side door. She faced Ty. "Okay, let's roll."

He held Morrissey under the armpits with his legs sprawled. "What the hell was that dance about?"

Instead of replying, she grabbed the dead man under the knees. "I won't be carrying my share of the weight like this. Let me get him around the middle."

Morrissey's blood smeared her khaki uniform. She should have put on her windbreaker; Ty was smart to do that. They stumbled a few steps toward her vehicle.

A burst of gunfire echoed against the canyon walls. She looked over her shoulder toward the road in front of them. Through the smoke, she saw the shapes of two men diving across from the right side to the left where the green sedan had run into the cottonwood trunk.

Ty's reaction was immediate. He dropped Morrissey, ducked behind her car and yanked his Beretta from the holster. "Take cover, Sam."

Her brain wasn't so agile. It took a few beats to register the obvious. Somebody was shooting at them. She needed to return fire, needed to find cover, needed to move. *Move!* But she stood there like a statue, holding the lower half of Morrissey's legs. She looked down. His sneakers were untied.

Ty's voice wakened her. "Sam, move! Damn it, move!"

She dropped Morrissey and bolted like a jackrabbit, dashing to her SUV, where she whipped open the driver's-side door to use as a shield. A bullet pinged against the door. If she'd been standing in the open, she would have been hit in the center of her bulletproof vest. Thank God she was wearing it today.

In the academy and during other training exercises, she'd been in dozens of simulations. But this was her first real-life firefight. As she drew her Glock, her focus tightened. Time seemed to slow. She remembered what was supposed to be done. *I can do this.* Her confidence returned and with it came courage.

When she spotted a backpack in the middle of the road where the two men had been, she yelled to Ty, "The hikers, these guys have got to be the hikers. The marshal said there were three."

From the opposite side of her SUV, he shouted, "I saw only two."

The hikers continued to lay down a steady barrage of gunfire. That was a lot of ammo. She regretted using her storage for a second ammo magazine as a carryall for latex gloves. Ty was aiming at a big, chunky boulder that was about ten yards down the road. She guessed the hikers would try to move toward the wrecked sedan, where they'd have a better angle.

Bracing her gun hand against the window frame of her vehicle, she popped a bullet into the space between the rock and the sedan. The action of her Glock felt good in her hands. She was a fairly good shot, the best in the Swain County Sheriff's Department…which wasn't saying much, given that Caleb was second best.

"Cover me," Ty yelled.

Peering through the space between her car door and the windshield, she fired in the direction he'd been shooting. Every bullet counted. She squeezed the trigger seven times, rapid-fire. Her ears rang with the percussive noise.

In a low crouch, Ty darted to the right side of the road, concealed himself in a ditch and took aim. He fired several times in quick succession.

A man staggered out from behind the boulder into the road. With one hand, he clutched his gut. Blood spilled through his fingers. With the other, he tried to steady his weapon. Ty fired again. The man crumpled to the dirt.

One down, two to go. She saw the second man run from the cover of the boulder toward the cottonwood tree where he could hide in the shrubs behind the car. He was closer to her than to Ty. Keeping her head down, she maneuvered toward the sedan.

The heavy smoke hanging over the trees made her think of a battlefield. Adrenaline pumped through her veins. She was on high alert, shivering and sweating at the same time. She dodged around the body of Morrissey on the ground. Her gloved hand touched the trunk of the sedan. She saw the hiker beside the tall cottonwood.

Ty ran toward the sedan, blasting as he came. She raised her weapon, took aim. She had the best angle—a head shot that was perfectly aligned. Before she could squeeze the trigger, the hiker was hit. He threw both arms in the air as he fell. *Two down, one to go.*

She could have sworn that shot came from behind her, uphill to her left. But when she looked, she didn't see anything but a couple of ragged-edged boulders and a dark wall of pine trees. Squinting, she tried to catch the glint of sunlight off a rifle barrel. If there was a mysterious marksman, he'd have to be using a high-powered rifle. A handgun wouldn't be accurate from those trees.

"Are you okay?" Ty called out.

"I'm fine. You?"

"There's another hiker, right?"

When the wind rippled the tall buffalo grass, she glimpsed him in her peripheral vision. He was half up the hill toward the trees. His pistol aimed directly at her.

She wheeled to face him. Somebody else fired first, and his bullet hit the hiker in the upper right chest. The hiker let out a fierce scream. He turned on wobbly legs and stared uphill to the point where she'd been looking. Then he went to his knees and curled up on the ground, moaning.

She rushed toward him, kicked his gun out of his reach and unhooked her handcuffs from her belt. With his shoulder wound, it seemed cruel to force the hiker onto his belly, but she wanted to be sure he was subdued and no longer a threat.

Breathing heavily, she got a lungful of smoke and coughed before she called out, "Ty, have you got the other two?"

"The one in the road is dead. The other is unconscious. I secured his wrists with a zip tie."

Her attack tally turned to a roster for emergency care: two wounded and two dead, including Morrissey. It was time to call for an ambulance. Proper procedure would have been to dial up the EMTs when they first discovered Morrissey's body. But she'd figured that the local emergency personnel would already have their hands full, being on call for the firefighters and treating patients with smoke-related illnesses.

As she reached for her cell phone, she looked uphill and saw a tall man in a cowboy hat with his arms raised over his head. This man had fired accurately through the smoke from a significant distance; obviously he was an excellent marksman. He was dangerous. She should have been scared but, for some reason, she wasn't.

She gave herself a mental slap. *Shape up, girl.* Just because he had his hands up, he was far from harmless. She could see the rifle strapped across his back and the two holsters on his belt. She lifted her gun and pointed it at him.

"Don't shoot," he yelled.

The sound of his voice sliced through her defenses and turned her insides to jelly. "Wade?"

It couldn't be. He was dead.

But that was her husband walking down the hill. She'd recognize his bowlegged gait anywhere.

He'd come back to her. Either that or she was dead, too. She must have been killed in this shoot-out, and her darling husband had come to greet her and escort her through the Pearly Gates. Their poor little Jenny was an orphan. She shook herself. No way. They couldn't both be dead.

Ty stepped up beside her. "This is what I've been trying to tell you."

"He's still alive."

"I'm afraid so."

She slammed her Glock into the holster, dug in with her toes and started running up the hill. There was not one single instant of hesitation on her part. Maybe she didn't know why he was back or where he'd been. But she didn't care. He was back. Wade was alive!

For a year and twenty-one days, her heart had been frozen solid. With one sight of him, the glacier shattered, and a warm, gentle feeling spread through her. As she ran, she heard the sound of her own laughter. Not a fake ha-ha but a real, bubbling, delighted sound. As she got closer to him, the smoke seemed to disappear. The whole world was bathed in golden sunlight.

With a giant leap, she flung herself into his arms. The equipment on her utility belt and her armored vest got in the way, but she did her best to have full body contact. Clinging to him with all her strength, she wrapped both legs around him. He felt different, more muscular. He felt right.

Her lips joined with his. There was nothing shy about their kiss. No clumsy fumbling around. No misdirected pawing. When it came to sex, they had always been good together. His tongue plunged into her mouth, and she welcomed the taste of him.

Neither of them was fresh and clean, and she should have been grossed out. Instead, it was the opposite. She nuzzled the bare skin of his throat inside his collar and inhaled his musky, manly aroma. Wade had never worn cologne, and that was fine with her. She liked the way he smelled.

His lips tickled her ear as he whispered, "I missed you, Samantha, missed you so damn much."

"Me, too." She kissed him again. "Where were you?"

"It's complicated."

She pulled her head back and stared into his light brown eyes. After a year and twenty-one days, after letting her think he was dead, he needed a much better explanation. "Tell me about it."

"There isn't time. I shouldn't have come down here, but I couldn't be this close and not touch you. You're an angel, so damn beautiful. But I've got to take off, can't stay here."

She wasn't letting him run away after giving her a whisper of sweet talk and "it's complicated." She needed a hell of a lot more than that. She slid down his body and planted her boots on the ground. "Sit down, Wade."

"I already told you. I can't—"

"We can do this the easy way or the hard way."

He frowned. "What?"

The hard way, it was. She stalked around him until she had the uphill position. From there, it was easy to shove his shoulder and hook his legs out from under him. As soon as his butt hit the dirt, she was on him. After taking away his rifle, she flipped him onto his belly and cuffed his hands behind his back.

"Wade Calloway, you're under arrest."

Chapter Four

Wade should have known better than to think he could pop back into her life and erase the past with a hug and kiss. He needed to do more, a lot more. But what a kiss! Her lips were delicate soft pillows but her need was hard. Her tongue had tangled with his for an aggressive battle that drew him closer, deeper.

Remembering, he licked his lips. A single kiss from Samantha was better than a week in bed with most women.

He rolled to his back and sat up with his legs stretched out in front of him. After Samantha pulled both guns from his holsters, she stood a few feet away and gave him *The Look*.

An involuntary grin tugged at the corners of his mouth.

"What's so funny?" she demanded with her arms folded across her chest.

Maybe he was still giddy from that amazing kiss, but *The Look* amused him. She meant for her scowl to be menacing, to strike terror into his heart. Instead, he saw a strong, sensible woman who was plenty ticked off but fair enough to hear him out.

"A question," he said. "What are you charging me with?"

"Let's start with attempted murder, two of them." Her

eyebrows pulled down, and her full lips thinned into a straight, angry line. "That was you, shooting from the trees."

"Let's call it self-defense," he said. "More accurately, defense of you and Ty."

Right on cue, his old pal tromped up the hill. "We could have handled it."

"You're welcome," Wade said.

"Incorrigible," Samantha growled. "The least you could do is pretend to be sorry. You have so much to apologize for, Wade. Not just to me but to all your friends, all the good people who showed up at your memorial service. Your sister couldn't stop sobbing, and she claimed to be glad your parents were dead so they wouldn't have to go through this tragedy. And then there's Jenny."

He watched *The Look* fade from her face, replaced by an empty gaze and vacant sadness that could never be fully expressed. When she spun on her boot heel and walked away from him, it was a knife in his heart.

She muttered, "I can't stand to look at you."

"Samantha, wait." He heard the desperation in his voice. "I can explain everything."

As she continued to put physical distance between them, she straightened her shoulders. "Ty, I'm going to contact Dispatch and tell them we need an ambulance, maybe two. Keep an eye on our suspect."

Wade's head dropped forward on his chest. Earning Samantha's forgiveness was going to be harder than hell. It was one thing to say that he'd faked his death so she and Jenny would be safe, and another to prove it.

"You're in big trouble." Ty hunkered down beside him on the hill. "Consider yourself lucky that all she did was throw you on the ground and slap on the cuffs."

The handcuffs were mostly a joke between them. Long ago during a particularly wild session in their bedroom, he'd shown her how to pick these locks. With his hands still behind his back, he dug into his pocket for the Swiss Army knife he always carried. His gaze locked with Ty's. He wanted to trust this guy he'd known since high school, wanted to believe that Ty was on his side 100 percent. Ty was one of a handful of lawmen who knew Wade had faked his death. He'd been nothing but supportive. But Wade had been betrayed by others. He had to be careful.

While he opened the knife and went to work on the cuffs, he said, "Kind of a coincidence, don't you think?"

"What are you talking about?"

"You and Samantha just happened to be on this particular stretch of road. You just happened to find Morrissey's body."

"Accusing me? Really?" Ty sat back on his heels. "You're a real piece of work, Wade. Do you really think I'd put Sam in danger?"

He wasn't sure what he thought or whom he believed in. "How did you get to be here? In this particular spot?"

"I sure as hell wouldn't call down an ambush on myself."

"Tell me," Wade said.

"Sam received a call from the fire marshal, who told her that the chopper pilot spotted three hikers near Horny Toad Creek. The marshal couldn't spare the manpower to pick them up, so Sam volunteered, since we were in the area."

Ty's story sounded plausible and bore no resemblance to the conspiracy theories that were running rampant in

Wade's head. It wasn't likely that the pilot, the marshal and Ty were in cahoots. Still, he said, "And why were you and Sam in this area in the first place?"

"I asked Sam to come with me while I checked out the safe house. And, yes, I had an ulterior motive. As soon as I heard about your escape, I figured you'd hightail it back here. And I wanted to warn Sam, maybe even take her and Jenny into protective custody."

"The hell you will." The pocketknife he was using to pick the cuffs slid across the metal and nipped into his thumb. "I know what protective custody is like. I'm not putting my wife and child through that."

"How are we going to keep them safe? When word gets out that you're alive, the cartel will use them. They'll threaten harm to your family unless you turn yourself over to them."

Wade wasn't sure how many people knew that he was still alive and waiting to testify against a former DEA agent and a member of the Esteban cartel who were in prison awaiting trial. He was the witness who could make sure those men were convicted of murder, conspiracy, drug trafficking and gun smuggling. His testimony would seal the deal…if he lived long enough to get into the courtroom.

"I've got a bad feeling," Wade said. "I think too many people already know."

"Is that why you broke out?"

"You make it sound like a great escape."

"Wasn't it?"

"Nothing so dramatic," he said. "After this last trip to the federal courthouse in Austin where—as you know—the trial was delayed for the seventh time, I went back to the safe-house motel with my handlers. Later that night, I climbed out the bedroom window."

"You just quietly sneaked out, huh? I heard you knocked both guards unconscious. One of them has a bad concussion."

"Not true. I wouldn't hurt anybody."

Ty cast a cynical gaze at the carnage spread across this smoky mountain meadow. "Yeah, you're a peaceful pussycat."

"I'm telling you that if my handlers were injured, I didn't do it. Whoever hit them could have been after me."

"None of the people who know you're alive have reason to want you dead."

Wade thought differently. Three days ago in Austin when he was leaving the courthouse, he caught a glimpse of a face he'd seen before. He didn't know the man's name but seeing him set off alarm bells. He needed to get back here, back to Samantha and Jenny as quickly as possible.

He regarded Ty with a steady gaze. His friend's easygoing manner was well suited to his ranching background, but Wade wasn't fooled for a minute. This laid-back cowpoke could move as fast as a rattlesnake's strike. Ty was sharp and smart. He was a good man; he'd earned an FBI Shield of Valor for his work on a kidnapping case.

The question was: To trust him or not to trust him? Even if Ty was brave and loyal, he was also a federal agent who wouldn't want to risk his job. "I'm going to ask you for a favor, Ty."

"Shoot."

"Don't tell anyone you saw me today."

Vertical worry lines creased between his brows. "That's asking a lot, brother. Those guys you shot are going to mention the mystery rifleman. And the forensic investigators are going to find bullets from the rifle."

Wade nodded toward the gun on the ground. "There it is. You can say that you were using it."

"You got it from the safe house, didn't you?"

"The rifle and two handguns," Wade said dismissively. There were more important issues at stake. Yes, he'd breached the sanctity of a federal safe house. So what? The place was never used. "I'm asking you for twenty-four hours. By nightfall tomorrow, I'll know what I need to do."

"I knew you spent the night in the safe house. As soon as I walked through the door, I could see that the dust on the floor had been disturbed."

"Yeah, yeah, yeah, and I ran water in the sink. And I ate a can of beans, left a dirty cup and messed up the sheets in the bedroom. Sue me." He heard a tiny click as the lock on his cuffs sprang open. "I need you to focus. Will you give me twenty-four hours?"

"If you can convince Sam, I'll do it."

Wade wished he was more sure of himself as he watched Samantha hike up the hill and stand beside Ty. Turning her profile to Wade, she spoke to his friend.

"My dispatcher contacted police and ambulance services in Glenwood Springs. They said they'd be here in half an hour, but I'm guessing it'll take longer. We need to do as much first aid as we can."

"I'll work on the guy by the sedan. And I'll get a tarp from your SUV to throw over Morrissey's body. His lieutenant is on his way. He'll want to see that we're showing respect."

"Even if Morrissey doesn't deserve it," Wade put in.

"Truer words never spoken." Ty backed down the hill. "I'm going to leave you two alone now."

Her thumbs hooked in her belt, she tilted her head down and stared at the buffalo grass beneath her boots. She'd left her hat in the SUV, and he noticed that her braided chestnut-brown hair wasn't as shiny as it used to be. Still beautiful but a little bit thin, her hair looked as if she hadn't been able to spend much time taking care of it. Managing the responsibilities of the sheriff's office was a lot of work.

A new wave of guilt splashed over him. Though he'd made sure that all her bills would be paid, he'd left her with a lot of loose ends. "Samantha?"

Her lower lip stuck out in a pout. "What?"

Her features weren't as tense as they'd been before. The deep sorrow had faded. The anger was gone, too. With a shock, he realized that he couldn't read her mood. They used to be in perfect harmony, perfect understanding. He'd lost that connection.

"Samantha, look at me."

She slanted a gaze in his direction. "I don't know what to do."

He swung his arms apart and made a grand gesture to show the cuffs dangling from his left wrist with the right side completely free.

"Ta-da!" He jumped to his feet. Like a magician, he took a bow. "The Great Wade has escaped the surly bonds."

Her blue eyes twinkled as though she was about to laugh. Instead, her chest heaved and a harsh sob exploded through her lips. In reaction, she slapped her hands over her mouth.

He caught her before she could run away from him. Gently, he peeled her hands away from her face and brushed a kiss across her knuckles. Her mouth trembled as she held back tears.

"It's okay," he murmured. "Everything is going to be all right."

Sobs overwhelmed her. He gathered her close and cuddled her against his chest, holding her shoulders while she poured out a torrent of tears. He patted her shoulders and stroked her hair, her silky-soft hair that smelled of flowery shampoo in spite of the fire and the smoke.

More than anything, he wanted to tell her that he loved her. This was the wrong time, too soon. And he was scared. Wade Calloway wasn't afraid of much. He was tough enough to take on a dozen rotten cops and a drug cartel, but he knew that Samantha could destroy him. If she denied his love or had given up on loving him, he might as well be dead.

"I have to go," he whispered to her. Ty had mentioned an officer with the state patrol was on his way, and then there would be the ambulances.

"I know." Her deep shuddering sobs had subsided to sniffles. Using his shirt, she wiped her face. "I heard some of the stuff you were telling Ty. You want to keep up the pretense that you're dead."

"And if the wrong people know I'm still alive and kicking, you and Jenny could be threatened." Her nose was red, and her cheeks were puffy from crying, but he thought she looked adorable. "You can't tell anybody you saw me. Within twenty-four hours, I'll have this straightened out."

With her right hand, she reached behind her back.

Keeping her voice low so Ty wouldn't overhear, she showed Wade his fancy Colt .45 with copper-inlaid handle. "I found this in the car with Morrissey, and I'm guessing it was put there to throw suspicion on you."

"Good guess." He took the gun from her and stuck it into his belt at the small of his back. "You kept this gun locked up at the house, didn't you?"

She nodded. "They must have broken in to get it."

A thief had violated the home he and Samantha had built together, their sanctuary, the house where their daughter slept. "Did you notice the break-in?"

She shook her head. "Half the time I leave the doors unlocked."

"That stops now," he said. "You can't trust anyone. Understand? Not anyone."

"What about Ty?"

Much as he hated to cast suspicion on his friend, Wade would rather err by being too cautious. "Trust him but keep your guard up."

"Of course I would. Ty told me a whopper of a lie about my husband being killed in the Roaring Fork River. Oh, wait, you told me that very same lie." Her bloodshot eyes narrowed. "Can I trust you, Wade?"

"I'll make this up to you. I promise."

"Not what I want to hear." She gripped the front of his plaid flannel shirt with both hands and pulled him close. "You need to listen to me, listen hard. You've spent a year trying to handle this by yourself. Don't make that mistake again."

"What do you mean?"

"You need me." She released his shirt and stepped back. "You need my help."

She was right. During the past year, Samantha had

proved she was capable of taking care of herself, their child and the entire population of Swain County.

He couldn't ask for a better partner.

Chapter Five

Sam's first-aid kit was suitable for scraped knees and poison-ivy rashes. Not life-threatening injuries. She knelt beside the unconscious man with the shoulder wound, which she had managed to bandage while still keeping his hands cuffed behind his back.

Wade had slipped out of his cuffs easily, which was as she'd expected. Arresting him was more of a symbolic gesture, a way of showing him that she refused to be ignored and would never be kept out of the loop again.

She still couldn't believe it. Her husband was back. He was alive. She wiped the smile from her face and tamped down her sense memory of how his arms felt when he embraced her and how his lips tasted when they kissed. *Not now!* She had to wait, couldn't allow her emotions to run rampant. And the anticipation was making her as edgy as a prairie dog surrounded by lawn mowers.

Her focus needed to stay on the practical aspects of how to handle his return from the dead. He'd promised to talk to her later tonight. The waiting was hard, but she believed him when he said it was necessary. And he'd spoken of possible danger to Jenny.

A worse brand of anxiety sped through Sam's veins when she thought of her daughter. Jenny was her precious girl with jagged bangs across her forehead that she'd cut all by herself and a strong singing voice that the church choir director said was remarkable. If anything happened to her precious five-year-old daughter...

Sam's attention returned to the injured man. He wasn't bleeding badly, but his chest heaved as though he was struggling for breath. A punctured lung? Internal bleeding? Where the hell were the ambulances?

If he died, it was her fault. Never mind that she hadn't fired the bullet that caused his wound. It didn't matter that the injured man was trying to shoot her and Ty before he was brought down by the expert marksmanship of her husband. Sam was the sheriff; therefore, she was responsible.

A fat lot of good all her training did. Yes, she was certified in CPR. Yes, she'd taken dozens of first-aid classes from the Red Cross. She'd heard of sucking chest wounds and septic shock and all sorts of emergency treatments for all sorts of injuries. However, until this moment, she'd never had to test those procedures.

She needed help. Why were the ambulances taking so long? She had to get out of here, had to get back to Jenny.

She stood and called to Ty. "I've got an idea. We could forget about the ambulances, load these guys into my SUV and drive them to the hospital. It'd be faster."

He was in the road, standing over the first man he'd shot, the dead man. In his gloved hand, he held a wallet. Though she was at least thirty feet away from him, she heard him muttering under his breath. Angrily, he wheeled around and shook the wallet at her. "Do you know who this guy is?"

How could she possibly know? "I'm sorry. Why should I recognize him?"

"Do you ever look at the BOLOs we send you?"

A bunch of law-enforcement offices, ranging from the FBI to the local Fish and Game warden, sent out computer notices or faxes of APBs and BOLOs to "be on the lookout" for certain license plates or vehicles or individuals. She always took a look at them and often hung them on the bulletin board. Ultimately, they became scrap paper that she handed to Jenny, who drew pictures with crayon or marker on the back. Passing a BOLO to her kid wasn't something she'd mention to Ty. She'd once caught Jenny drawing lipstick and purple eye shadow on a felon's mug shot.

Her ears pricked up as she heard the sound of a motorcycle engine cranking to life. Ty had heard it, too. He glared up the hill toward the place where Wade had disappeared into the trees.

"Oh, that's just great," Ty growled.

"A motorcycle," she said. "Why is that a problem?"

"I'm guessing that your husband swiped a very nice little Honda from the safe house. A good bike, it's got heavy tread for off-road and goes a decent speed on the highway."

"He wouldn't have taken it if he didn't need it."

"But it belongs to the FBI."

"Don't even think about whining. I had to dig deep into my sheriff's department budget to buy disposable smoke masks, and the FBI can afford to leave an entire house standing empty."

"Point taken." His tone became more conciliatory. "I just hope he doesn't wreck it, that's all."

She walked down the hill toward him. "Let's get back to what you were talking about. Tell me who our dead man is."

"Tony Reyes," he said. "He works for the Esteban cartel, and he's on the short list of Most Wanted for both the US and Mexico."

She'd heard horror stories about the drug cartels: beheadings, torture, brutal murders of women and children, and human trafficking that amounted to a slave trade. Never in her wildest imagination had Sam thought she'd be in contact with this type of criminal. Swain County was a lazy little territory with one semicharming town and a couple of local ranches. Nothing ever happened here, and that was the way she liked it.

"Why does this Reyes person rate so high on the Most Wanted list? What has he done?"

"He's an enforcer. He kills people, especially cops."

Like Morrissey. The murdered state trooper lay at the side of the road covered with a tarp. If the smoke hadn't already been blocking the sun, she would have sworn that the day turned darker.

She hated the way these pieces were falling into place. Had Reyes been the one who took Wade's gun from her house? Did he know where she lived? "Are these the people Wade is testifying against? How did he get mixed up with a drug cartel?"

"It's worse than that, Sam."

"Worse?" Her frustration erupted in a burst of absurdities. "What could be worse? Vampires? Zombies? Oh, wait, maybe Wade actually is dead and he's the zombie."

"What?" Ty looked concerned.

His frown made her laugh. Her grandma always said that nothing was so terrible that you couldn't laugh about it. *Oh, Granny, you're so wrong.* For the past several months, Sam had few reasons to giggle. Even now, after learning Wade was alive, her chuckle sounded a little hysterical.

As she paced up and down on the road, she indulged in wild speculation. "Let me see, what could be worse? Did Wade do something to upset the Nazis or the terrorists or, maybe just maybe, he's being pursued by undead Nazi zombies."

"Are you done?"

She paused by her SUV, leaned forward from the waist and rubbed at the two bullet holes in the driver's-side door. "This has been a lot for me to absorb. First, I've got a dead husband who isn't dead. Then I find out that my daughter might be in danger. And now you're talking about drug cartels."

"It's more than drugs. There's also evidence of human trafficking. A cache of high-tech weaponry was discovered, thanks to information from Wade."

The scope of these crimes sobered her. They were dealing with very evil, very scary people. "Is this as bad as it gets? Is there more?"

"Rogue cops," he said. "Wade witnessed criminal acts and transactions between the cartel and law enforcement. We're not sure how far the corruption spreads."

"Is that why you and Wade hated Morrissey?"

He nodded. "My boss is running the task force. They were keeping an eye on Morrissey, hoping he'd lead us to others. And there are a lot of others. Cops, patrolmen, inspectors, DEA agents, maybe even FBI agents, who are taking kickbacks from the cartel."

Literally, there was nobody she could trust, nowhere she could turn for help and no way to escape. The idyllic time in her life was over. When she and Wade were first married, they'd been so happy while building their house, having a healthy baby and making their dreams come true. Now the future looked a hundred times more complicated.

Ty had his cell phone in hand. "I need to tell my boss about this."

"Wait." She stopped his hand before he could lift the phone to his ear. "You aren't going to tell your boss about Wade, are you?"

"Come on, Sam, you can trust him. Everett Hurtado is a decent guy. Kind of a bureaucrat, he probably won't even come out here into the field."

"You promised Wade." She'd overheard that much. "You gave him twenty-four hours."

"Like I told you, Hurtado is running the task force. He already knows Wade is alive and escaped from custody. He's the one who suggested I come up here and poke around at the safe house."

Also to make contact with her. If his boss had been looking for Wade, it stood to reason that Wade would be drawn to his family and would show up in Swain County. Ty's SSA might not be as upstanding as he thought. "Your supervisor doesn't know where Wade is. You can't tell him. Not until tomorrow."

"Okay, fine."

This was important. She stuck out her hand and pinned him with a gaze. "Deal?"

When he shook her hand, he gave an extra little squeeze. "If I didn't know better, I'd think that you and Wade were out to ruin my career."

"Maybe I am," she teased. "Then you and Loretta would have to move back here and go to work on your daddy's ranch."

"The twins would love that."

He turned away to place his phone call, and she saw the red and blue flashing lights from a Colorado State Patrol vehicle—a Crown Vic, silver with a blue-and-black dash and a logo. Most of the staties were nice guys who were willing to do the paperwork on traffic citations, but she was seeing law enforcement through a different lens. Both Ty and Wade had agreed that Morrissey was corrupt. Why not his boss?

She'd never particularly liked Lieutenant Trevor Natchez. When it came to appearances, he was one of the most by-the-book officers she'd ever met. His white-blond hair had a short military cut. His shirts were always crisp. The dark stripe down his beige trousers was never rumpled. According to rumor, he washed his vehicle at least once a day. His vocabulary, however, was gross. It always surprised her that someone with such a high regard for cleanliness could talk so much filth.

Natchez swore constantly. Whenever she was around him, Sam used a mental (bleep) so she wouldn't be distracted and wouldn't show him that his bad language bothered her. He enjoyed irritating her and never failed to come up with borderline sexist comments when they met. Given those ugly characteristics, she halfway expected Trevor Natchez to be up to his elbows in dirty dealings.

After he parked his vehicle behind hers, he climbed out from behind the steering wheel, straightened the flat brim on his uniform hat and strode toward her.

"If it ain't Little Miss Sheriff," he said with a sneer. "What happened to my man Morrissey?"

She glanced around him to look at his car. The inescapable dusting of ash from the fire must be driving him nuts. "You left your flashers on," she said. "Were you hoping to keep the crowd at bay?"

"When I want advice from you, honey, I'll ask for it."

She directed him to the tarp, squatted beside it and held back the corner to reveal Morrissey's face. The folds of his chin were slack. His skin had taken on a grayish hue. Sam couldn't stand the dead man's stare and had pulled his eyelids down.

For a brief moment, Natchez seemed shaken. He clenched his jaw, and his thick blond eyebrows lowered so much that she couldn't see the blue of his eyes. He flipped the tarp to cover the dead man's face and tilted his head upward. While he scanned the skies as if looking for heaven behind the clouds and smoke, a litany of profanity spewed from his mouth.

"Where did you find him?"

"In this car." She pointed. "Shot in the chest, he was behind the wheel, but there wasn't any spatter. He must have been killed somewhere else."

"Did you come up with those conclusions all by your cute little self?" He glanced at Ty. "Or did this FBI stud help you?"

Ty ended his phone call and greeted Natchez with a pat on the back and a handshake. The two of them were as friendly as could be. They stood over the body of their fallen comrade and said a few things about what a truly great guy Morrissey had been, quick with a joke, sharp as a tack, a credit to the uniform, blah, blah, blah…

Earlier, Ty hadn't been so complimentary. He'd as much as told her that Morrissey was under suspicion for working with the cartel. She supposed Ty's conversation with Natchez fell into the "never speak ill of the dead" category.

Natchez scanned the area. His gaze paused on each of the dead or injured men. "What happened here? Did our sexy lady sheriff pitch a fit?"

Her hand rested on the butt of her gun. It would have given her great pleasure to shoot this man between the legs and ruin his perfectly neat uniform. "We were ambushed."

"No way."

"My dispatcher has already put in a call to the ambulances," she said. "They should be here any minute."

"Who told you to move the body?"

"Nobody had to tell me anything," she snapped. "These murders were committed in my county, and I have jurisdiction over the investigation."

"The heck you do. Morrissey was my man. I should be the one who looks into his murder."

She got in his face. This was one of those times when Sam was glad for her giraffe-like height. Natchez was an inch or two shorter than she was, and she made it seem like even more by stretching her neck and straightening her shoulders. "Here's the deal, Lieutenant Natchez. The investigation is mine. But I'm aware that I don't have the facilities to do thorough forensics."

"Damn right you don't."

"Neither do you. The state patrol doesn't have a coroner. You can't do an autopsy."

He opened his mouth, no doubt to swear, but nothing came out. Maybe Swain County was too small and too limited in resources to handle this case, but Natchez wasn't equipped for doing a murder investigation, either.

"I suggest," she said, "that we request assistance from the FBI on these cases."

"Good plan," Ty said as he held up his cell phone. "I just talked to my supervisor, and he mentioned the same thing."

Natchez gave a nod. "I'm okay with that. If you need my help, I'll do whatever I can."

Ty asked him, "Is losing a man going to cause you any problem in scheduling?"

"To tell the truth, Morrissey was cutting back on his hours. He used more sick time than a teenage girl getting out of gym class with the cramps."

She turned away. Where, oh where, were the ambulances? There was no hope of providing sensitivity or enlightenment to Natchez. She tried to ignore him, but he was like a rash that wouldn't stop itching.

Natchez swaggered around the scene with Ty. They paused beside the dead man on the road, whom Natchez recognized immediately from a BOLO. Well, of course he would. The guy probably had every notice on file going back ten years, probably practiced with them every night like flash cards.

"I heard a rumor, Ty. Maybe you can verify. I heard that Wade Calloway is still alive."

Too much! Hearing her husband's name on the tongue of this bigmouthed jerk sent Sam right over the edge. In a couple of quick strides, she was beside Natchez. With her right hand, she yanked his wrist behind his back, putting a nasty crease in his shirtsleeve. Her left hand held her stun gun at his throat.

"Never speak of my husband again, unless you intend to humbly and without profanity praise him for being an American hero. And show some respect for me, the grieving widow."

"Yes, ma'am."

Finally, she'd got through to him. All it took was an outrageous act of violence on her part.

Chapter Six

When Sam drove past the supermarket on the east edge of Woodridge, she noticed more activity than usual in the parking lot, and she wondered why. Typically, if a blizzard was predicted, everybody rushed to stock up on food and necessities. The fire might be having the same effect, even though gathering more supplies wasn't a good idea if your house might be burned to rubble.

On the wide main street that went through the center of town, every slanted parking space was taken outside the diner, the coffee shop and the two taverns. This was something she understood. People liked to huddle together and reassure each other when trouble was near.

She wished that she could do the same.

But she couldn't talk about Wade's return from the dead or the possible danger from a criminal cartel. Not even Ty knew the whole story; she hadn't shown him Wade's gun that had been planted in Morrissey's car. Besides, Ty wasn't here. He'd gone with the ambulances. One would deliver the wounded to the hospital in Glenwood Springs. The other would transport Morrissey and Reyes to wherever their bodies would be autopsied.

Sam was alone with her problems.

Somehow, she had to cope.

After a stop at the one traffic light in town, her SUV cruised past the Swain County Courthouse, where the 911 dispatchers were babysitting her daughter. Sam's bloodshot eyes bored a hole in the two-story building, wishing she could see through the chiseled red stones to where her daughter was drawing or skipping rope in the wide corridors or sitting at a desk and rearranging the clutter.

Before she picked Jenny up, Sam needed to be certain that her house was safe from intruders. Somebody had sneaked inside to steal Wade's revolver. They might come back, might want to grab her to get to Wade. Worse, they might come after Jenny.

The threat to her daughter enraged her, made her as fierce as a mama grizzly. But it also terrified her. Was she tough enough to keep her child safe? Sam couldn't take that chance; she needed to get Jenny far from harm's way.

Luckily, the solution was obvious: her dad was a captain in the Portland, Oregon, police department. Sam had already called him and arranged for Jenny to visit Grandma and Grandpa. The approaching fire provided a good excuse for sending her daughter to safety, while she herself stayed here and helped Wade investigate.

About six miles outside town, she made a left onto a curvy asphalt road that she paid extra to have cleared by the snowplow in the winter. Now, in springtime, the drive was green and pleasant with the new growth of shrubs and leaves sprouting on the trees. Runoff from the snowmelt made a sparkling rivulet in the ditch beside the road.

After her SUV passed the neatly lettered sign that marked Kendall's Cabin, her nearest neighbors, she drove around a stand of aspen to the two-story log home that she and Wade had built. The peaked roof above the second floor covered a balcony that stretched across the front of the house and provided shelter for the wraparound porch. A huge cedar deck jutted from the south end of the house outside the kitchen. At this time of year, she and Jenny usually ate dinner at the picnic table on the deck, where they could watch the hummingbirds zoom around the hanging feeders filled with red-tinted sugar water.

She could hardly wait until Wade joined them again. He loved cooking on the grill with the flames leaping high—maybe he loved the flames a bit too much. His burgers were usually burned. Her nose twitched as she remembered the charred aroma of her husband's cooking.

They were about to become a family again. Or were they? He had betrayed her in the worst imaginable way. How would she ever forgive him?

In her parked car, she sat and gathered her thoughts. Before her husband supposedly died, she'd never thoroughly appreciated him. Wade had always been affectionate, giving her pats on the butt and subtle hugs and surprise kisses on the nape of her neck. She'd yearned for those gentle touches almost as much as she missed having him in her bed.

Her life had been shattered by his fake death. She'd gone through the steps of grief from denial to anger to bargaining to depression to acceptance. Now she was back to anger. She flung open the car door. She needed to take action and not stew in her own fury. Her number one chore was to make sure the house was safe for Jenny.

Just in case there was somebody lurking, she drew her weapon as she climbed the three stairs to the wraparound porch. Had she remembered to lock the door this morning? No, she hadn't. The handle turned easily. She silently chastised herself for being too complacent as she stepped over the threshold.

Nothing appeared to be disturbed in the living room. Some of Jenny's stuffed animals were arranged on the plaid sofa as though they were watching television. A long bar with tall stools separated the kitchen from the living room. The dining room was to the left of the kitchen and the deck was to the right through the sliding glass doors.

She prowled across the hardwood floors. On the kitchen bar, there was a note, written in crayon. It said, "Great minds think alike. The house is all clear. Lock the front door. Come to the bedroom." Instead of his signature on the bottom, Wade had drawn a cross-eyed green frog.

Sam holstered her gun, charged across the room to the entry, where she'd already flipped the lock. She climbed the stairs two at a time and pushed open the door to her bedroom.

The extra-long four-poster bed with the denim-blue comforter dominated the room. She didn't see him, but her husband's black cowboy hat was hanging on the post nearest the door. She unbuckled her heavy utility belt and draped it over a chair. Then she took off her hat and perched it on the post opposite his.

"I remembered," she said. "Never put your hat on the bed."

He came out of the adjoining bathroom with a pair

of pliers in his hand. "Hat on the bed is bad luck. Don't know why, don't know how, but that's the fact."

Before he could set down the pliers, she pulled him into her arms and planted a firm kiss on his mouth. The taste of his lips and the feel of his hard, sinewy arms wakened all her senses and made her feel truly alive. It was as though her nerve endings had been paralyzed and were now—suddenly and provocatively—reconnected. Electricity sizzled through her. She could almost hear the pop and crackle as the tension that had held her captive for one year and twenty-one days released.

He swung her in his arms, lifting her feet off the ground while their lips were still joined. The dark anger lifted. Pure joy bubbled up, and she couldn't hold it inside. She broke the kiss, threw back her head and laughed. When he waltzed her backward and shoved, she easily toppled onto the bed.

"Wait." She lay on her back, holding him off with both arms. "What did you mean when you said something about great minds thinking alike?"

"When I left you by Horny Toad Creek, my first thought was about Jenny. I needed to make the house safe for her." He pushed one of her arms out of the way. "I knew you'd do the same thing."

He was correct. Not a surprising conclusion given that they both loved their daughter more than anything in the whole world. She fended him off with one arm. "How'd you get here so fast?"

"I rode cross-country on that Honda I swiped from the FBI safe house. My route was likely faster than going the long way around on the regular roads. That's why I beat you home."

"Plus, I had to wait for Lieutenant Natchez and the ambulances."

"I thought you'd have to go all the way to Glenwood with the wounded," he said. "The crimes were committed in your jurisdiction. That means you're in charge, right?"

Of course he'd see it that way. He'd been sheriff for nearly ten years and handled things mostly by himself. That wasn't her way. She took her responsibilities seriously and did as much as she could. But if somebody else could do it better… "I don't have the resources to investigate a murder. No forensic laboratory. No CSI team. And the county coroner is a dentist. I handed jurisdiction to Ty and the FBI."

His mouth tensed. "You did what you thought was best."

He would have looked angry, but a couple of dimples appeared amid the stubble on his cheek and softened the chiseled lines of his face. His light brown eyes, a color that reminded her of champagne, sparkled. His flash of anger was gone. She knew exactly what was on his mind.

She sat up on the bed and pushed him away. "There are a few things we need to discuss before this goes any further."

"I don't mind talking, but make it fast." He held her chin and darted close for a quick little kiss. "Please make it fast."

When he stepped away from her, she felt his absence. Her fingers itched to trace the ridges of his abs and tweak the hair on his chest and tangle in his rumpled brown hair. She needed to make love with him, to reassure her body that he was really here with her again. But she wouldn't rush things. This time, they played by her rules.

"I haven't forgiven you, Wade. You know I'm not the sort of woman who holds a grudge, but you destroyed me with your betrayal. It's going to take more than your handsome smile to patch this relationship back together."

He sauntered across the bedroom to the dresser, folded his arms and sat on the edge with his long legs stretched out in front of him. For a long moment, she just stared at that fine-looking cowboy, *her* cowboy. His shoulders were bigger than before and the sinews in his forearms were more sharply defined. He had big hands, big wrists.

He cocked an eyebrow. "Well?"

Discombobulated, she stuttered, "Well, w-w-w-what?"

"What's it going to take to make you happy?"

With a mental effort, she swept her thoughts into a pile and started with the most important. "It's about Jenny."

"I can't wait to see my girl."

"That's not going to happen." She braced herself for an explosion before she continued, "The only way I'll feel comfortable about her safety is if she's out of the area. I already called my dad. He and my mom are flying out here in his Cessna to pick her up."

Wade's disappointment was palpable. The pain of being separated from Jenny for more than a year had to be devastating. She wished it could be another way.

"What about tonight?" His voice was husky. "Just an hour."

"It'd do more harm than good."

"Does she remember me? What does she say?"

"She draws pictures of you, of all three of us. She makes portraits of a happy family that doesn't exist.

Not only does she talk *about* you, but she talks *to* you, like you're an imaginary friend."

He winced.

Though she wouldn't wish this kind of guilt and sadness on anyone, she needed him to be sensitive to his daughter's needs before he thought of himself. Jenny loved him, and that love hadn't changed when he was supposed to be dead.

Sam rose from the bed and paced across the room, showing him her back. Breathing hard to let off steam, she rubbed at her midriff. Her lungs were constricted by the bulletproof vest she wore under her uniform shirt. "You put us through hell, both me and Jenny."

"I'm sorry."

His voice was as faint as a sigh. She heard his sadness. But it wasn't enough, damn it, not enough. She whirled to face him. "I've overheard Jenny having a chitchat with her imaginary daddy about how Mommy isn't fair. And, guess what, she's right. Mommy's not fair. Mommy makes demands and enforces the rules. Mommy is always going to do what's best for her little girl."

He didn't contradict her. "What's best?"

"I don't want her to see you tonight and then be forced to leave you tomorrow morning. She doesn't deserve that sort of heartbreak."

She watched his Adam's apple bob up and down as he swallowed hard. "I hate what you're saying, but I understand."

"And you agree, right? Promise me you won't try to see Jenny tonight." When he didn't reply immediately, she added, "Not only is it bad for her, but the other problem is obvious. Jenny's just a kid. She won't be able to keep your secrets."

"You didn't tell your dad about me?"

"Hell no." Sam's overprotective father, Jake Lindstrom, would never approve of an undercover investigation with her mysterious husband who had faked his own death. "I told him that the fire was a strain on our resources in Swain County, which meant more sheriff work for me. And Jenny's regular babysitter had gone to Denver. Plus, all this smoke can't be good for a kid."

"And he likes any excuse to fly across the country in his pretty little five-seat aircraft."

Her dad had been a pilot in the navy and never lost his love of flying. His greatest extravagance was a Cessna 185 Skywagon, named *Lucky Lindstrom*, which was one of her dad's nicknames after he survived a supposedly lethal gunshot wound. He planned to use the Cessna for circling the globe after he retired from the Portland PD. Until recently, her mom had been rigidly unenthusiastic about his plans and refused to set foot in the plane.

"Mom has finally accepted *Lucky Lindstrom*, maybe because Dad allowed her to reupholster the seats and get her own pink headgear for talking to the tower. She's coming with him."

"When do they get here?"

"They'll fly into the Glenwood Springs airport tomorrow morning." Her dad would have made the trip without stopping overnight, but her mom liked to take it easy. "They'll call when they get in."

He crossed the room and took her hands. "You're right about the way we should handle this with Jenny. I can't promise I won't be watching my little girl tonight, but she'll never know I'm near."

"How's that going to work?"

"I'll find a way. You won't see me, but I'll keep an eye on you both, keep you safe while you sleep."

She liked the idea of being cared for, having her protector back on the job. "Like a guardian angel."

"Samantha baby, I'm no angel."

"Don't I know it."

He was the only person who called her by her full name. And he was definitely the only one who dared refer to the nearly six-foot-tall sheriff who wore a Glock on one hip and a stun gun on the other as "baby." The intimacy of those two words melted something inside her. Her defenses were gradually unraveling.

"Samantha." His tongue rolled over each syllable. "Let's go to bed."

She snatched her hands from his grasp. "I have other demands."

"Bring them on."

"First, let me do this." Her fingers flew down the front of her uniform shirt, unfastening the buttons. There was nothing erotic about this striptease. Her moves were purely practical; she needed to get the bulletproof vest off.

"Can I help?"

Unlike her, he was sexy. His voice, his eyes, his lips, even his dimples—the whole package was a major turn-on, except for one very important aspect…the smell.

"You don't get to touch me," she announced as she ripped apart the Velcro straps, "and I won't touch you." She tore off the vest and stood before him, wearing her bra and her boxy uniform trousers. "I usually like the way you smell, but we need to take a shower. Right now. Both of us."

In a flash, he was peeling off his clothes. "I had

planned to clean up before you got home, but I got distracted. That's why I had the pliers in the bathroom."

"To fix the leak," she said as she sat on the edge of the bed and shucked off her boots. The faucet in her bathroom sink had been dripping for over a month—just one of those chores she intended to handle but never found the time.

"I already had the toolbox out," he said, "and I figured it would only take a sec."

Oddly, his willingness to take care of a mundane household task was almost as exciting as his bare chest. This was how they had been for years as wife and husband, partners in life who managed the daily chores. And then, at night, they turned off the lights and got down to business. She didn't know why that familiarity was so very sexy, but it was. Her ability to resist him was completely undone. She stepped out of her trousers and into his arms.

He pulled her into the bathroom and turned on the shower. Steam rose in a moist cloud and wrapped around them. All day long, the smoke from the fire had assaulted her senses. This steam was soothing, healing.

Wade tugged off the last bits of their underwear. Again, this wasn't a smooth romantic moment. She didn't hear the strain of violins or feel the brush of an angel's wings. His actions were practical. *Getting down to business.*

Then he looked her up and down…slowly. At each place his gaze touched, her skin prickled, from her throat to the tips of her breasts to her stomach to the apex of her thighs. A shudder rocked her body. The determined control she'd used to manage her sensations and emotions shattered. His glance had set her free.

His cheeks dimpled when he smiled. "Can I make a demand?"

"You can try."

"Tomorrow morning, I want you to get on the Cessna with your parents and Jenny. Go with them. I want you to be safe in Portland until this is over."

Not a chance.

Chapter Seven

Sam didn't give him an answer. Not yet. Right now, while she and Wade were naked and facing each other, she didn't want to argue. It was time to savor the moment.

She closed her eyes, hoping to shut out all the responsible things she should be doing—finding the rest of the ventilator masks, investigating the murder of Morrissey, checking in with her deputies to see what troubles the fire had brought and rushing back to town to pick up Jenny from the courthouse.

Not now. She claimed this reunion with Wade for her own. *This is my time.*

Finally, she could be a woman again. When she'd first heard that her husband was dead, part of her had died, as well. She'd stopped noticing other men, didn't even try to flirt. She'd lost the desire to kiss, embrace or even touch. Now that Wade was back, she meant to make the most of their time together. They would be getting down to business…a lot.

Her eyes popped open. Undressed and unembarrassed, she stepped into the frosted-glass shower stall and turned around to face him again. As the steaming water cascaded down her spine, her appreciative gaze devoured the tall, handsome man who stood just outside the shower door. She couldn't decide whether she wanted to pull him closer and feel his body against hers or just stand here and stare, dumbstruck with admiration. He'd been working out. She could tell.

"While you were dead," she blurted, "I didn't date other men."

"It would have been okay if you did." He braced one hand against the edge of the shower door. "Don't get me wrong. I wouldn't be happy if you found a new boyfriend, but I'd understand."

"Would you?"

"I'd try, but then I'd probably kick his ass."

He stepped into the stall and closed the door. Though they'd designed the shower to accommodate their size and height, there was no way to avoid each other.

It's time. She was ready to make love. Or was she?

With her backside pressed against the green tiled wall beside the faucets, she felt strangely reluctant to touch him and seal the deal. Though she wanted him with every fiber of her being, this might be too much, too soon. Was it because she hadn't forgiven him? Or because he seemed to think she'd be willing to hop onto her father's aircraft and leave him to investigate alone?

She really wished he hadn't suggested that she run and hide. She wasn't a child. He seemed to be putting her in the same category as Jenny. Oh my God, Jenny! Sam thrust out an arm and reached for the shower door.

He caught her wrist. "What are you doing?"

"I need my cell phone from my trousers. What if Jenny calls and I don't answer? She'll be freaked out."

"I'll get it," he said firmly. "You stay here."

Her first instinct was to get the phone herself, the

way she'd been doing everything by herself. While he was gone, she'd been mother and father to their daughter. How could she trust anybody else to get it right? But she had to trust him. If she was going to bring Wade back into her life, she had to accept him as a full partner. "Okay, you go."

As soon as he left the shower, she felt his absence. During their separation, a chill had crept into her bones and taken up residence. What if he died again? Loneliness was never more than a heartbeat away. She was crazy to invite him back into her life while they were surrounded by danger. If something happened to him, if he left her...

The door to the shower opened, and he held up the cell phone. "There were no calls or texts. I'll put it by the sink."

She nodded.

He stepped back inside, close to her. With his thumb, he tilted her chin up and studied her face. "Were you crying?"

She honestly didn't know. "I don't think so. It's just spray from the shower."

"I hurt you, Samantha. And I'm sorry, so damn sorry."

"I know."

With one hand he stroked, slowly and rhythmically, up and down her arms. With the other, he picked up the tail end of her long braid. "Did you want to wash your hair?"

"Not enough time." Using a barrette she kept in the shower for precisely this purpose, she hurriedly fastened the braid in a knot on top of her head. "I'm not late to pick up Jenny, but I ought to leave soon."

"You're worried about her," he said.

"You bet I'm worried." She grabbed the soap and started lathering up. "Ty said that one of the men we shot was part of the Esteban cartel. Those guys are mad-dog killers."

"Jenny will be fine. Nobody knows I'm alive."

"The people you escaped from," she pointed out. "They know. And that jerk Natchez said he'd heard a rumor about you."

"What did you tell him?"

"First, I got the drop on him with my stun gun." She grinned at the memory. "I told him to show some respect for a grieving widow."

His laughter echoed inside the shower stall, and she felt herself beginning to relax. This man wasn't a stranger or someone she'd just met. He was her husband. They had a long history together.

He took the soap from her hand and turned her around. "Have you missed having me wash your back?"

"Maybe."

"Relax, Samantha."

She rested her arms against the tile wall while he massaged her shoulders and spine. His touch sent quivers of wild, exotic excitement across the moist surface of her skin. "Do you remember what you told me the first time we showered together?"

He spoke in a lecturer's voice. "In the western United States, water is a precious commodity. Even if the frequent droughts haven't affected the water flow or pressure, it's up to each of us to conserve water. I convinced you that getting naked was the environmentally aware thing to do."

"How could I refuse? I'm a total eco-slut."

He turned her around so the shower spray sluiced down her back to rinse off the soap. "I'd like to start on the front side. Those breasts look like they need a lot of attention. Do we have time?"

"We do if I don't leave tomorrow."

His gaze searched her face. "What?"

"I'm not leaving with my dad tomorrow." No matter how much she wanted him, she had to take a stand. "You need me. When you came up with the idea of faking your death and going into hiding, you cut me out of the investigation."

"I was protecting you and Jenny. Being stashed away in safe houses with bodyguards watching your every move isn't fun. I didn't want that for you and Jenny. I wanted you to have a normal life."

"By turning me into a widow?"

"The witness-protection thing was only supposed to last for a couple of months, but—"

"I don't want to hear it," she said. "The plan—whatever it was—didn't work."

His intention had been to do the best for his family. She believed that. But he and Ty and the FBI had gone about it all wrong; their scheme had turned into a mess.

"You're right," he admitted. "It's ended up with all of us being in danger while the bad guys are still at large."

The strangeness of standing here naked and discussing their situation had not escaped her. She was conscious of the tight nubs at the tips of her breasts and the hot water sliding over her hips. But she couldn't stop talking. The need for argument overwhelmed her. Instead of making love, she was stating her case. "Why did you choose this moment to make a run for it?"

"At first, I just wanted to grab you and Jenny and

disappear. After I found Morrissey dead and the other three men started attacking, I knew I couldn't let this go. I need to end the threat."

"Yes," she said with relief, "and I need to help you. Please, Wade. We can solve this together."

There wasn't enough physical space in the shower for him to escape her, but it was obvious that he wanted to put some distance between them. He turned his head to the side, avoiding eye contact. As if that weren't enough, he turned away.

And she didn't stop him.

She could hardly believe that she was here, naked and as horny as she'd ever been in her whole life, with the man she acknowledged as her soul mate, and she wasn't touching him, kissing him, not even grabbing his muscular ass.

Her breasts weighed heavy with desire. From low in her belly came a steady pulsating throb. *Do it, just do it now.* But she clenched her fingers into fists and drew back. *Not yet.* She hadn't forgiven him. And she was anxious about Jenny. And she needed him to accept her as a partner.

"All right." His voice was low and ragged. "We're a team."

Her impulse was to wrap her arms around him and press her body against him, but she held back. Instead, she glided her hand between his shoulder blades. "It's going to all work out."

He pushed open the door of the shower and stepped out. "After you finish up in there, you should pick up Jenny."

When he closed the door, she was alone in the hot-water spray with the steam whooshing around her. She'd clung to her reservations by refusing to forgive. She'd accepted her responsibilities, starting with getting her daughter from the courthouse. She'd stated her demands and won the argument.

And she was miserable.

WADE HAD HOPED to share dinner tonight with his daughter and wife. He'd hoped for laughter and for hugs. In the best of worlds, he would have had a T-bone on the grill, a cold beer in his fist and an old Johnny Cash song on the outdoor speakers. Instead, he was hiding, lying flat on his belly in a storage space amid the rafters in the garage. He'd widened a space between the boards so that he had a clear view of the deck on the south end of the house. The smoke didn't seem to be causing him a problem with visibility.

At half past five, the shadows grew long, but there was still plenty of daylight. Ten minutes ago, Samantha had parked her SUV near the front door, which was just beyond his range of vision. He'd asked her to bring Jenny out on the porch, and he waited anxiously to see his little girl.

He'd heard her voice. When they pulled up in front, she was belting out a song, "Let It Go." He had to wonder if her mom had coached her to warble that tune; it had meaning for him. He was the one who'd taken her to the movie, and they used to drive along in the car together, singing at the top of their lungs. His voice sounded like an elk's bugle during mating season, but his daughter was musically talented. He wanted to get her a piano... if Samantha ever let him back into the house.

Their argument in the shower had taken him by surprise, not that he expected her to forgive him right away.

He'd put her through hell, and he regretted every tear she'd shed and every sigh of longing that had passed through her soft, full lips. Though he was willing to spend the rest of his life making it up to her, he didn't know how many more incidents like the shower he could take without going crazy. You couldn't put a woodpecker in a redwood forest and tell him not to poke, couldn't expect a fox in the henhouse to go vegan. His wife was a sexy, desirable woman, and he was a man.

They'd been only seconds away from full-on sex. He'd been aroused. And she was, too. He knew her well enough to see the signs. She wanted him with all the frustrated, pent-up desire of being apart for over a year.

Then she'd stopped short.

From inside the house, a screeching alarm sounded. Had somebody broken in? Wade couldn't see the north side of the property. Instantly alert, he braced himself, wrapped his hand around the long barrel of his hunting rifle and prepared to drop from the rafters. Taking action would be a relief after all this waiting. Then his cell phone buzzed.

This was a burner phone, and only Samantha had the number. During his cross-country run after he escaped from the Texas safe house, he'd picked up half a dozen throwaway phones. She was calling him on the one he'd given her.

Her voice was loud in his ear. "How do I kill this stupid alarm? I tried the off button, but it doesn't work."

"It's not exactly state-of-the-art." He'd purchased the burglar alarm several years ago and stashed it away in the garage. Before she went to pick up Jenny, he'd finished hooking it up and shown her how it worked. "Did you unplug it?"

"Duh! Of course I did." In the background, he heard Jenny asking her mom about who was on the phone. Samantha replied to their daughter, "It's the guy who fixed this thing."

Jenny yelled at the phone, "Don't quit your day job."

He chuckled, "Did you teach her that?"

"Would you please focus? What do I do about this screaming thing?"

"It's got batteries," he said. "Open the panel on the bottom and pop them out."

The alarm went silent.

"Thank you," she said. "I knew there was a reason I never wanted this alarm hooked up."

"Uh-huh." From what he'd seen, she'd rather leave the front door wide open and roll out a welcome mat for intruders. "It's motion-sensitive. Promise you'll turn it on tonight before you go to bed."

"I'll think about it."

While he watched, the sliding glass door opened, and Jenny came onto the deck. She carried a sketch pad and a flat pencil box he'd given her. Humming to herself, she set down her drawing tools and climbed on top of the picnic table to check the red liquid in one of the hummingbird feeders.

His daughter was so remarkable, so beautiful that she took his breath away. Her thick brown hair, which was the same rich color as her mother's, hung straight past her chin. The front was cut with weirdly slanted bangs. When she looked up at the feeder, he could almost see the blue of her eyes. He wanted to be closer to her, close enough to count the freckles he knew were splattered across her nose.

He whispered into the phone, "She's taller."

"Growing like a weed."

When Jenny stood on tiptoe in her pink high-top sneakers, her T-shirt with a multicolored, shiny heart came untucked from her red skirt. A sparkly bracelet flashed on her wrist. Though she liked being a princess, his little girl could outrun and outswim a lot of boys her age.

When she started singing to herself, he was overwhelmed by a fierce longing. He clenched his jaw so he wouldn't open his mouth and call out her name. Earlier today, he'd watched Samantha from afar. Seeing his daughter was different, more primal and visceral. The way he'd handled being apart from his wife was to think about her all the time, to write her letters that were never sent and record messages that were never spoken. With Jenny, he shut down the "daddy" part of his brain… and his heart. He couldn't stand thinking of her and not being with her. He loved this child more than life itself.

"Samantha," he growled into the phone, "we need to get this solved right away. I can't wait much longer. I need my family."

"Soon," she promised.

As she disconnected the call, she came onto the deck. With her fists braced on her hips, her gaze scanned the surrounding forest and focused on the garage. When she smiled, he knew it was meant especially for him.

Chapter Eight

Throughout dinner, Sam knew that Wade was watching. His voice on the phone had sounded so desperate that she almost called him back and invited him to join them. Not a good idea.

If Jenny saw her daddy, she'd never allow herself to be bundled off to Portland, even with the very special bribe of being able to ride in Grandpa's little plane and a promise that she didn't have to go to school. Jenny needed to go with her grandparents, to get away from here, to be safe.

And so, Sam didn't signal her husband. He could *not* join them. Later, there would be time for them to be a family again. For now, he could only watch. Having him as an audience made her feel self-conscious, as if the deck on the south end of the house was a theater stage and she was standing in the spotlight.

While serving their spaghetti dinner, she found herself striking poses that showed off her long legs in skinny jeans. On top, she wore a floaty tunic in a lavender print. This might be the most flattering outfit she owned. Her legs were most definitely her best feature, and the long tail on the tunic covered up her too-skinny bottom.

After slurping a long spaghetti noodle, Jenny stared across the picnic table. "How come you're all dressed up?"

"I'm not." She glanced toward the garage. Though she couldn't see Wade, she figured he was there. The storage area under the slanted garage roof made a good hiding place.

"Are too," Jenny said. "You never wear that shirt unless you're going someplace special."

"I've been slogging through smoke and yuck all day," Sam said. "After I took a shower, I felt like putting on something nice."

"Do you have a date?"

"What?" Sam had zero social life. "Why would you ask that?"

Jenny shrugged. "There's something weird about you."

At age five, Jenny was just beginning to be embarrassed by her mother. Though she enjoyed the perks that came from having her mom be sheriff, she had told Sam many times that she hated the uniform. If Jenny had her way, all the sheriff's badges would be bedazzled with pink rhinestones. But that wasn't going to happen anytime soon. Sam was still the mom, still the boss, and she didn't need to explain herself to her daughter.

She cleared the dinner plates. "As soon as we're done here, we'll get you packed."

"We have to fill up the hummingbird feeders. I betcha the fire makes them hungry."

"I bet you're right."

The devastation of the forest would affect the local fauna, from the tiny birds to the black bears and mountain lions. No matter how civilized the mountains were, this was still a habitat. Nature came first.

After filling the feeders, she checked her email and talked to the dispatchers at the courthouse. Then she personally contacted each of her six deputies and informed them that they'd be on call until the fire was completely contained. The real reason she needed her team to step up was so she'd have the time to investigate with Wade. But she couldn't come right out and say that Wade was back; telling the truth was not an option. Nor did she dare to attempt a cover story. Sam was a terrible liar and wouldn't be able to hide her excitement about Wade's return from the dead. Deputy Schmidt sounded suspicious and didn't like that the FBI had taken over the investigation of the murders. She'd cut him off midsentence and ended the call.

When this was over, there would be fences to mend. It occurred to her that when this was over, Wade would be back, and he might want to be sheriff again. And she might want to step aside and let him take over. That would be a huge change. Though she welcomed the extra time to be with Jenny and to work on the house, she'd miss wearing the badge and having folks depend on her.

As soon as she went through her evening rituals with her daughter and got Jenny tucked into bed upstairs, Sam heard a car pulling up in front of the house. It was just after nine o'clock, which was a little late but not outrageous.

In usual circumstances, she wouldn't think twice about charging onto the porch, but a touch of paranoia slowed her step. Why hadn't this visitor called first to let her know they were coming? Since she'd followed Wade's suggestion about pulling all the curtains after dark, she had to peek around the edge of the window. A dark blue truck parked next to her SUV. In the glow from the porch light, she saw Justin Hobbs, the fire marshal, climb down from the driver's side.

Her fears dissolved in a puff of smoke, which was kind of appropriate for a fire marshal. Though she didn't know Justin well, he had a reputation for being a reliable, stand-up kind of guy. When he wasn't in the midst of an active fire, he tended to be unassuming and to fade into the woodwork, even though he was a big man with a barrel chest and a full black beard.

Before he knocked on her door, she opened it and held her finger across her lips to indicate quiet. "Do you mind if we talk outside? I just put my daughter to bed."

Chagrined, he mimicked her finger-across-the-lips gesture. "Sorry, Sam, I should've called first."

"You've got enough on your plate." She led him around to the deck, which was on the opposite side of the house from Jenny's bedroom. Reaching inside the sliding glass door, she turned on the porch light so that Wade could see and hear what was happening, and she wouldn't have to explain later.

She turned to Justin. "Tell me about the fire."

"It's still burning but seventy percent contained."

From the edge of her deck, she looked toward the southeast, where the night sky was tinged with an ugly red haze. The flames weren't visible from here, but their destructive light colored the smoke and blurred the stars. "I thought we were expecting rain tonight."

"I'm still hoping," he said. "I wanted to let you know that a couple of properties are in the path of the blaze."

His calm demeanor told her that there weren't people living in the cabins. Still, the idea of a house going up in flames disturbed her. "Where?"

"They're near the place called Hanging Rock."

"Eyesores." She knew the exact location. "One of them is missing half the roof. Windows are broken. The wood siding has aged to a dead gray. If those houses burn, I say good riddance. They're probably haunted, anyway."

"Do you believe in that stuff?"

She gestured for him to have a seat. "Can I get you something to drink?"

"I'm fine." He held up a half-full water bottle as he sank into a chair. His bulk filled the rough wood frame, but she wouldn't describe him as being overweight. He was big. "And you didn't answer my question. How about it, Sam? Do you see ghosts?"

When she heard about Wade's death, she'd tried to contact him on the other side, even consulted with an Arapaho shaman. There hadn't been a tiny glimmer of awareness. But, of course, he hadn't really been dead.

"I'm not sure about ghosts," she said, "but the local high school kids like to sneak around those deserted houses looking for some old-time prospector. Hanging Rock is a prime location for parties."

"I guessed as much. I sent a couple of my firefighters down to check the houses out, and they reported finding a lot of junk and discarded beer cans."

"Are the houses still standing?"

"Yeah, and they might survive the fire, depending on which way the wind blows."

She sat in the chair across from him, close enough that she could smell his heavy cologne. Like her, Justin had changed from the clothing he'd worn all day while working near the fire. He probably used the cologne to mask the stench of smoke.

"Anyway," he said, "it might be a good idea to track

down the property owners and notify them of the situation."

"No problem. I'll pass that task to the clerk at the courthouse."

They sat in silence for a long moment. She wondered why he drove here to deliver the message personally when he could have called. The poor man looked as if he was struggling to keep his eyes open.

He snapped his thick fingers. "I almost forgot. I brought you a box of disposable ventilator masks. They're in the back of my truck. Twenty-four of them."

"Thanks so much." She reached over and gave his knee a friendly pat. "I started off the day with a box of my own but gave them all away."

"How's your little girl?" He leaned forward. "Does the smoke bother her?"

This was a good opportunity for Sam to try out her first lie about Jenny. "Actually, the smoke is kind of a problem for her, and her regular babysitter had to take her little boy into Denver. The poor kid has asthma."

So far, so good. The first lie was out there: Jenny was having trouble with the smoke. That wasn't such a stretch.

"Sorry to hear that," he said.

The second lie, which was more complicated, stuck in her throat. She didn't want to tell anybody that Jenny was going to Portland; bad guys could buy plane tickets to Oregon. She needed a different destination. "I'm going to send my daughter to stay with a friend of mine in Denver for a few days."

"Woodridge is perfectly safe. I can guarantee that."

"Getting my daughter out of town is partly for me," she said. "Worrying about the fire while taking care of the other things a sheriff needs to do is making me real tired."

She clamped her lips shut to keep from doing any more talking. Most lies fell apart because the liar kept embellishing until nothing made sense. "Yep, I'm exhausted."

"You do a fine job as sheriff. Everybody says so."

"Well, thanks."

"Do you mind if I ask you something personal?"

He stretched out his long arm and did exactly what she had done, placing his huge hand on her knee. She didn't get a sexual vibe, but his touch was more intimacy than she wanted. How could she refuse to answer his question? It seemed rude. Maybe if she ignored it, the question would go away. "I want to thank you for the way you kept me informed today."

"That's my job."

Right off the top of her head, she couldn't recall if Justin was married or not. She thought not. And he wasn't wearing a wedding band. She scooted forward as though getting out of her chair. "I'll go with you to your truck so I can pick up those masks."

"Sam, you've been a widow for over a year. As far as I can tell, you're not seeing anyone. Is that right?"

Before this nice man could go any further, embarrassing them both, she took his hand in both of hers. "It's by choice, Justin. I'm not dating anybody because I'm not ready to move on. I'm too much in love with my husband."

"Wade was a good man."

"Sometimes, I feel like he's still close to me, still watching over me."

Justin rose from the chair. A very big man, he matched

Wade in height and was far more massive. "I appreciate your honesty."

"Let's go get those masks."

She glanced toward the garage, where she suspected Wade was hiding. Even if he wasn't physically close, she hadn't lied to Justin Hobbs about her feelings. Wade was her soul mate, the only man she would ever love. That was truth.

WADE SWUNG DOWN from the rafters and crept from the garage toward the front of the house, where he watched Hobbs and Samantha saying their goodbyes near his truck. Hobbs towered over his tall, slender wife and was as wide as two of Samantha put together. Though Wade was in excellent physical shape, he was glad he wouldn't have to wrestle with Hobbs to win Samantha's love.

She loved him. Good to know. She wouldn't let him near his daughter and threatened to throw him out of the shower, but she still loved him. And he felt the same.

They needed to dig into this investigation and get things figured out soon, real soon. Having Hobbs drop by turned out to be useful. He'd said something that provided Wade with a starting point.

Samantha waved farewell to the fire marshal who had the hots for her...no pun intended. As she strolled back to the front door, she was humming, not paying attention at all to her surroundings. If somebody came after her, she wasn't ready.

"Samantha," he hissed from the shadows at the side of the house by the wood box. "Over here."

"What are you doing?" she whispered back. "Jenny is upstairs, and if she sees you..."

"She won't. I've been watching."

"From the garage, right?"

It was the most obvious place. He wasn't about to give her a prize for guessing correctly. And he didn't plan to push his advantage and insist on coming into the house, where he could sleep comfortably. For tonight, he'd patrol outdoors and make sure his family was safe. Starting tomorrow, he and Samantha would start investigating.

"I set up that alarm for a reason," he said.

"To make me crazy?"

"Protection." He kept his voice low. "These are dangerous men, Samantha. If they knew I was alive, they'd use you to get me to do whatever the hell they wanted. They know I'd lie for you and Jenny. I'd commit treason. I'd kill for you."

"You're scaring me, Wade."

"That's the idea."

He'd meant to lecture her on taking safety precautions and staying alert. But when she was this close, his physical need overruled his brain. He clasped her upper arms and pulled her deeper into the shadows, into the darkness.

His kiss was gentle for about three seconds. Then she moaned. His mouth pressed harder against hers. His tongue pushed past her teeth and tangled with hers.

He started dragging her closer but stopped himself. If her lean body pressed against his, he didn't trust himself to be prudent. He'd tear off their clothes and make love to her right here in the open with no thought of the possible consequences. He was so damn weary of being cautious. He wanted his woman.

First, he wanted her safe.

He ended the kiss and spoke in a rush. "Go inside and set the alarm. I'll be out here watching tonight."

"Okay."

"What time do you take Jenny to the airport tomorrow?"

"Early," she said. "I talked to my dad, and he said they'd be here around seven thirty or eight."

Good. She'd been smart to make arrangements with her father, who was a cop and a man who loved gadgets. The security at his house in Portland was top-notch. Leaving early in the morning made it unlikely that the bad guys would take notice, and he'd overheard the story she'd told Hobbs. "Are you telling people that Jenny is in Denver?"

"In Denver with a friend of mine. That should be vague enough to keep anyone from looking for her."

"You lied to Hobbs. Do you have any reason to suspect him?"

"Justin?" Her voice must have been louder than expected because she clapped a hand over her mouth. "I barely know him. We're just friends."

"It sounds like he wants to be more than friendly."

She leaned so close that her breath tickled his ear. "He's not the only one."

Being around her was torture, pure and simple. He ached with need for her. He couldn't stand breathing in the scent of her lavender soap, hearing the teasing lilt of her voice and feeling her skin, her silky skin. Her full, soft lips taunted him. If he kissed her again, he would surely lose all control.

"Get a good night's sleep, Samantha." He took a backward step away from her. "Don't look for me tomorrow. I'll find you, and we'll get started."

Hobbs had given him the location where they would start. The place where Wade had witnessed a crime was near Hanging Rock.

Chapter Nine

Sunrise painted the clouds and smoky haze with eerie shades of blue and gray, slashed with streaks of yellow and red where the sun tried to break through. As Wade rode away from the airport in Glenwood Springs on the safe house's motorcycle, he thought of the old saying: *red sky at morning, sailors take warning*. Though he was nowhere near the sea, he needed to be careful. *Take warning*. No one could be trusted. There was more than his own safety at stake; Samantha would be with him as soon as she dropped off Jenny and headed back in this direction.

For the nine hundredth time, he considered the risks involved in working with her. She was a decent markswoman, an experienced cop and smart at figuring out puzzles. Those attributes counted as pluses. She had one big minus: Samantha was gullible. With a big smile on her face, she wanted to believe that everybody was good at heart and that nobody lied or cheated.

Before he got to the airfield, he turned the bike onto a side road and drove about a hundred feet to a thick stand of aspen trees on a hillside. He saw no other vehicles and doubted that anyone was following him. Why would they? Nobody but Ty knew about the bike, and

Wade's helmet disguised his identity. Still, just in case he felt threatened, he'd left himself a back-door escape; he could take off through the forest on this sweet little Honda.

After he dismounted and stretched his legs, he looked down at the crossroads. Samantha would take this route back to Woodridge, and he figured he could catch her along here. If her father landed when expected, Wade had less than a half hour to wait.

He took out one of his burner phones and put in a call to Ty. His old pal's voice sounded puzzled when he answered.

"What's the matter?" Wade asked. "Didn't recognize the number?"

"Burner phone," Ty guessed. "Where are you?"

As if Wade would answer that question. "What happened at the hospital?"

"Two dead, two survivors. Both of the men who made it are low-level thugs associated with the Esteban cartel. Both have criminal records. Both are from Denver. And, wonder of wonders, neither of them mentioned seeing you. They barely noticed me."

They were both watching Samantha. He didn't blame them. "Are you still at the hospital?"

"That's not how the FBI works, my friend, and you know it. Give us a murder and we swing into action like a well-oiled investigative machine."

They were a machine, all right. But the feds weren't always a model of efficiency. Wade had experienced a year's worth of glitches while they tried to mount their case. Most of the agents, like Ty, were effective lawmen, but others were half-assed losers, like the two guys who were supposed to be watching him at the safe house and let him slip out a window. Well-oiled? No way.

Ty continued, "We've got CSIs going over the car, which is not—as we suspected from the lack of blood spatter—the primary crime scene."

"He was shot somewhere else."

"Correct," Ty said. "Autopsies are scheduled for this afternoon in Denver. And I left an agent at the hospital to keep an eye on our prisoners. It'll be another day or two before they're ready to be transported."

It was too much to hope that the thugs would provide useful leads or make a deal with the feds to inform on their colleagues. These guys were low-level. If they ratted out their bosses, the cartels would take extreme revenge. Still, Wade asked, "Did you get anything from questioning them?"

"The two survivors claim to be working for the one who died. They know nothing."

"Probably not far from the truth," Wade muttered. "Where are you?"

"My dad's ranch." Ty's voice brightened. He loved coming home. "This is our command central. My SSA is coming up this afternoon to coordinate the investigation."

If Supervisory Special Agent Everett Hurtado was getting involved, it meant something bigger than Morrissey's murder was going down. "What's SSA Hurtado looking into?"

"For one thing—" Ty lowered his voice "—he wants to find you. I don't know how long I can keep you out of this. If Hurtado asks me directly, I can't lie to his face."

Though Wade didn't want to broadcast his location, Hurtado was one of the few who already knew that he'd faked his death. The SSA still belonged in the "do not trust" category, but keeping Wade's whereabouts a secret from Hurtado wasn't worth Ty losing his job. "You can tell him, as long as he understands that I'm not going to turn myself in or go back into custody."

"Why not? We can all work this together."

During his time in protective custody with nothing to do but think, Wade had run through many scenarios. No matter how he looked at the smuggling operation, one conclusion remained the same: someone in law enforcement was the ringleader, and it wasn't the DEA agent who was already in prison. This ringleader, the big kahuna, kept the other dirty cops in line and saved the Esteban cartel from getting arrested.

Was Hurtado the ringleader? Wade didn't know, couldn't be sure. "You said that nabbing me was one thing Hurtado wanted. What are the others?"

"Only one other," Ty said. "Something big is going down real soon. It has to do with weapons being sold to the cartel. Big guns were stolen from a US Army arsenal outside Colorado Springs, stuff like rocket launchers and bazookas."

He couldn't drag Samantha into the middle of this war. But he couldn't leave her alone to fend for herself. "We've got to put an end to this. How did Hurtado hear about the weapons deal?"

"I don't know."

"When does it happen?"

"Again, we're not sure. The fire might have thrown off the timing. These cartel boys are secretive. They don't like making a move when there are choppers flying overhead and firefighters swarming across the landscape."

Wade had to think Hurtado was getting his information from a snitch. Morrissey might fit that bill. If he was passing secrets to the FBI and some of the bad guys found out, it was a sure motive for murder. "What can you tell me about Morrissey? Did you get any leads from his death?"

"We've got no suspects. Following procedure, I talked to Sam last night and filled her in on the details."

In her role as sheriff, she needed to stay apprised of the situation. The crimes had been committed in her county. While Wade was gone, Ty had kept him posted on how Samantha was doing as sheriff. *Stellar* was the word he used most often. Not only did she keep a lid on the few crimes that happened in Swain County, but she'd instituted new programs for helping the homeless and dealing with domestic violence. She was also involved in educating the kids about the dangers of drugs, which was a topic that had got complicated after recreational marijuana was legalized in Colorado.

According to everything he'd heard, she was a damn good sheriff. The last thing he wanted to do was usurp her authority.

He made one last stab. "Anything else you can tell me?"

"Not a thing, nada."

Wade wasn't sure if Ty was holding back or just didn't know any of the details. SSA Hurtado was running the show for the FBI, and he wouldn't want Ty stealing the spotlight. Hurtado didn't have much use for Wade, either.

Sooner or later, they'd have to confront each other. Wade wasn't looking forward to seeing Hurtado at the ranch. He said goodbye and ended the call.

Seated on the Honda, he waited for Samantha to

come chugging along the road in her SUV. Without the smoke, this would have been a spectacular spring day with the breeze ruffling through the green aspen leaves that would turn to golden coins in autumn. A shaft of pure sunlight cut through the clouds and the haze to splash against a jagged pillar of granite that stood like a sentinel at the edge of the forest.

His memory cast back to another spring day when he'd walked among these white aspen trunks and listened to the wind rattling in the leaves. Wade had lived almost his whole life in Swain County. He knew the terrain, the landmarks and the houses. The inhabitants changed from year to year, but there were those who still remembered when Wade and his younger sister and the Baxter kids dashed around like a pint-size gang. A far cry from a drug cartel, their most reckless prank was turning loose three chickens inside the house of their rival.

Deputy Caleb Schmidt was the one who caught them. He still hadn't stopped teasing Wade about the stunt. For Wade's thirtieth birthday, Caleb presented him with a chicken-shaped cake. Foolish pranks and small disagreements were the norm for Swain County. Not arms deals and smuggling.

He spotted Samantha's SUV. Only a few other cars and trucks had used this back-road route, and no one appeared to be following her. He waited an extra minute, watching, and then he zipped down the hill on the Honda and turned onto the road behind her.

Though his motorcycle wasn't built for high speeds, he had no problem catching up with her thirty-five-mile-per-hour pace. Samantha was an excellent driver, better than him, and she maintained a steady, unflappable speed while he rode up beside her window and flipped up the face mask on his helmet.

She grinned and shouted something he couldn't hear over the noise of the engine. He gestured for her to follow him. In about seven miles they'd be in Swain County. Four miles after that was a turnoff. If nothing had changed in the year he'd been away, the turnoff would lead to a small farmhouse and horse barn that was occupied only in summer. When he was sheriff, the family who owned the place asked him to check in occasionally to make sure they hadn't been vandalized. He'd never found a disturbance at this remote property.

He parked his bike on the far side of the barn where it wouldn't be visible from the road. Samantha parked in the same area. She left her car and rushed toward him, talking as she approached.

"I had a dream about you," she said. "You were holding my hand and dragging me toward Hoppy Burger in Grand Junction, the place that has a rabbit with huge ears on the logo. But you weren't wearing a shirt. And I kept telling you—no shoes, no shirt, no service." She came to a halt in front of him but didn't stop talking. "By the way, you look really hot in that leather jacket."

"You're pretty hot yourself. I like you out of uniform."

"I can tell you've been working out. It shows in the abs."

"There wasn't much else to do."

"Okay, back to my dream. At Hoppy Burger, I told you that you couldn't go in. And you pointed to me. I looked down. And I wasn't wearing a shirt." She tossed her head, and her long braid whipped back and forth.

"Here's what I think it means. You're breaking the law, and now I'm about to join in your life of crime. Think so?"

Retelling dreams wasn't something he did, but he liked to hear Samantha talking and to see a sparkle in her big blue eyes. He slipped an arm around her slender waist. Without the bulletproof vest, her body was soft, feminine and pliant. She molded herself to him.

"It means," he said, "that you want to get naked with me."

"No deeper meaning? No complex interpretation? You think I just had a sex dream."

"Baby, that's the best kind."

As she snuggled closer and nuzzled the crook of his throat, his pulse thumped faster and louder. Wade was a grown man who ought to have self-control. But as soon as she touched him, his reaction was about sex and nothing else. The blood drained from his brain and rushed to his groin. He was hard. His hand slid down her back, pausing at the flare of her hips and then gliding down to cup her bottom. He adjusted her position until she was rubbing up to him in exactly the right way.

She whispered, "I'm ready to make love."

The thrill that ripped through his veins nearly knocked him off his feet. Those were the words he wanted to hear from her, but he hadn't expected her to say them so quickly. He thought there would have been more discussion, probably another apology on his part. He'd been prepared for a long talk about Jenny and her parents and the Cessna. Only after that would they move on to sex.

Her direct approach was different.

He didn't complain.

"This way." He took her hand and led her through a

side door into the horse barn—a long building with a center aisle and stalls on either side. He turned on the lights, which were just a couple of bare bulbs. The barn felt musty from being closed up, but the smell wasn't bad if you didn't mind hay, leather and horses.

He climbed a wood ladder to the loft, and she followed. When he opened the hinged window that overlooked their vehicles, a cool breeze swept inside. This area above the stalls was tidy but not spotlessly clean.

Her boot heels clunked as she paced on the bare, unvarnished wood floor. "Does anybody live here?"

"In the barn?"

"On the property, smart guy."

"The owners don't usually return until June." He crossed the loft and took her hand. This would be their first time together in over a year; he should have taken her somewhere classy. "This old horse barn isn't good enough for you."

"What did you have in mind?"

"Like on our honeymoon. We stayed at that five-star hotel in Hawaii."

"My best memories of that week aren't about the champagne and orchids and fancy sheets." She tossed him an over-the-shoulder glance and ran the tip of her tongue over her top lip. "I remember getting dirty with you in the jungles and sandy on the beach."

"Are you telling me I didn't have to pay for all that luxury? Would you have been just as happy wearing flip-flops and sleeping under the stars?"

"Don't get me wrong. I love the deluxe treatment." Her voice lowered to a sexy growl. "But I don't mind making love in a barn with the right man."

This warm, sexy version of Samantha spurred him

into action. He didn't want to wait too long and give her a chance to remember how angry she was with him. In a storage cabinet, he found a variety of camping equipment stacked on wide shelves. He rummaged through the gear and dragged out two sleeping bags, which he unzipped and spread on the floor. He peeled off his leather jacket, folded it and placed it at one end for a pillow.

The bed was made. He sat back on his heels and flashed a smile. "Join me."

"How did you find this place?"

"The same way I find everything. I was out wandering and stumbled upon this house and barn." He smoothed the sleeping bag. "I've slept here before."

"When?"

He sensed a shift in her mood. The urgent sexy Samantha had taken a step back. "I've known about this loft since I was a teenager. If I hadn't been able to use the safe house, I would have come here."

"Since you were a teenager, huh? Have you ever brought other women to this loft?"

This was not a discussion he wanted to have. Not when they were so close to reconciliation. Staying on his knees, he took her hand and held it to his lips. "There are no other women."

"Good answer."

"I know."

She rewarded him with a grin. "I have a feeling that no matter where we went, you'd be able to find shelter, food and a quiet place to make love. You know every inch of Swain County."

"Am I that predictable?"

"Not in any way." Finally, she lowered herself into

the nest of sleeping bags. "A man who fakes his death, spends more than a year in protective custody and then escapes from the FBI is not a stodgy old stick-in-the-mud."

The first thing they took off was their holsters. He placed both of their handguns within easy reach, which might be a mistake given the way her temperament was fluctuating between seductive and scary. They both pulled off their boots. She shucked off her denim jacket, and her fingers went to the top button on her blue-striped shirt.

"Wait," he said. "Before we take off our clothes, there's something I want to do. May I unfasten your braid?"

In answer, she turned so she was facing away from him. He held the length of her shining brown hair in his hand. At first glance, the color seemed to be a simple brown. Further study revealed shades of deep mahogany and shimmering strands of gold. He unfastened the band at the end of the braid and started spreading the long strands across her back.

"This is turning out okay," she said.

"It's all good." Her hair, like liquid silk, slipped through his fingers.

"We're a team, investigating together. When do we start?"

"Soon." He pushed aside the curtain of hair and leaned close to nibble her earlobe.

"When?" she demanded.

His focus wasn't on crime solving. All he wanted was to savor the taste of her body, inhale her clean scent and caress the perfect softness of her skin. "Later today, we need to meet up with Ty at his ranch."

"Uh-huh."

"But we start at Hanging Rock."

Chapter Ten

Hanging Rock. The two words rattled ominously in her head. Last night, the fire marshal had mentioned properties at Hanging Rock that were in danger of burning, and Sam was certain that Wade had been listening. What could possibly be of interest at Hanging Rock?

"Those houses," she said. "Nobody lives there."

"Where?"

"Hanging Rock."

"I can't do this." His stroking of her hair abruptly ceased. "I can't split my attention. Either we talk about the investigation or we make love."

"I want both." She twisted her head and looked over her shoulder so she could see him. "First, love. Then investigate."

"I can do that."

His focus switched from her hair to the task of separating her from her clothing. He pulled her across his lap, kissed her mouth and opened her blouse. Of course, he didn't do all those things at the same time, but the way he shifted her from one position to the next was smooth. She was still reveling in one set of sensations when another started up. He went from her lips to her chin to her breasts to her throat, her shoulder, her elbow.

He was everywhere at once. It was as though he had magic fingers.

While her breasts were tingling from his kisses, he spread her knees and unzipped her jeans. Magic fingers were inside her pants. Her breath caught in her throat and her skin prickled and her muscles flexed and relaxed in a throbbing crescendo as he teased her to a shuddering release she hadn't felt in over a year.

She exhaled a contented moan. "I'm so glad I chose sex first."

"We're not done."

"Good." To be completely honest, she couldn't stop thinking about sex when she was with him. This morning when she'd awakened with a gasp, she'd been completely aroused. Her dreams were—as he suggested—more about sex than anything else, and she was ready to re-engage that part of their relationship exactly as it was before.

Forgiving him would be harder. She was leery. Though she didn't think he'd deliberately misled her, she could see him pushing her out of the investigation in a misguided attempt to protect her—similar to the way he'd faked his death to keep her and Jenny safe. What kind of lunatic reasoning was that?

She held his face in her hands and stared deeply into his copper-brown eyes. There was more to their relationship than just sex. They'd built a home and a life together. They had a child. But the sexual component was overwhelming. It always had been. From the very first time she'd laid eyes on this tall, lanky cowboy with the dimples and the lazy smile, she'd wanted him. And vice versa. On their first date, they'd spent the night together, and she wasn't that kind of girl.

She whispered, "I never could say no to you."

"Yesterday in the shower," he said. "Was that the first time?"

Her head bobbed. "That should give you an idea of how angry I was."

She doubted she could resist him again. Her first orgasm was only a taste of what she knew would happen later. With Wade in control, she was in for a spectacular ride.

Again, he started with her hair. His hand tangled in her long mane, which he twisted into a knot at her nape. She couldn't move without causing her hair to pull. Slowly, slowly, he brought his mouth closer to hers. His kiss started as a light peck. His tongue flicked against her lips, teasing her. When she tried to move, he tightened his grasp on her hair, making sure she stayed exactly where he wanted her. His gentle nibbling became more demanding. The pressure increased. He tugged at her hair, pulling her chin up. His kiss was hard and savage. He took her breath away.

Breaking free of his grasp, she flung herself into his muscular arms. She wanted to be part of him, wanted him inside her. Under his skillful direction, they shed their jeans. In seconds, he had them positioned on the sleeping bags. He poised above her, ready to enter.

Though almost unconscious, she managed to speak. "Wait."

His body tensed. "Why, Samantha?"

"We need a condom. I'm not on the pill anymore."

Having sex with anyone else had been unthinkable for her. She'd quit worrying about birth control.

He grabbed his jeans, took out his wallet and produced a plastic-wrapped packet. "I came prepared."

But he hadn't mentioned the condom until she brought it up. Wasn't he worried about an unwanted pregnancy? Maybe it wouldn't be unwanted. While he was supposedly dead, she'd thought about having more children. She wanted Jenny to have a younger brother or sister... someday.

For right now, all her needs and desires were wrapped up in the man who parted her thighs and entered her slowly. When they joined, her inner walls clenched around him. In moments, they began the familiar yet wonderful rhythm of their mating.

His deep, rich voice murmured in her ear, "I love you, Samantha."

She couldn't stop herself from saying, "I love you back."

Giving her trust to him was a very different matter.

SAM WOULDN'T HAVE minded making love again and again, but Wade had only the one condom, which he'd purchased in a men's bathroom, just in case. The idea of having unprotected sex and possibly making another baby was in her mind, but there were too many other things to discuss, and she was anxious to start their investigation.

Basking in the afterglow, she was too comfy and content to leave their sleeping-bag nest, but she'd put on her blouse to ward off the chill in the horse barn. Wade had slipped into his jeans. She noticed that he was going commando.

"Before we get started at Hanging Rock," she said, "I have some questions."

"Me first," he said. "How was Jenny this morning? Was she okay about going with her grandparents?"

"Okay but not thrilled. Sometimes she's a little fussbudget, worrying about everything, from which stuffed animal to pack, to which pills she needs in case she gets airsick."

"Does she get airsick?"

"Not a bit." Sam didn't know where Jenny had heard about airplanes making your tummy jump; must have heard it from one of the kids at school. "And she worries about leaving me alone."

"Ouch." He winced. "Kids shouldn't have to feel that way."

"It's natural. She thinks you're gone and I'm the only family she's got left. If she loses me…"

"I understand."

She knew how deeply he connected with those feelings. Wade had lost his father to cancer when he was twelve. He and his sister were raised by a hardworking single mother—an unsung heroine in Sam's opinion. That gracious lady lived long enough to hold her granddaughter in her arms. Her death in a car accident nearly broke Wade's heart.

His eyebrows crinkled in a frown. "I never should have put you and Jenny through this."

Though she agreed, there was no reason to rub salt in his wounds. "My first question—what exactly did you witness?"

Stretched out on the sleeping bag with his fingers laced behind his head, he gave her an optimum view of his bare chest. "I've told this story a couple hundred times to the cops and lawyers. It probably sounds like a police report."

"Then it ought to be clear."

"I responded to a late-night call from the dispatcher at nine forty-four and took care of the problem. I was—"

"Hold up. What problem?"

"Mrs. Burroughs."

Thelma Burroughs was a sweet old woman who'd lost her husband two years ago. Ever since, she'd been hearing burglars, vandals and escaped convicts prowling around her property. Her calls to 911 came three or four times a month.

"Funniest thing," she said. "After you disappeared, I assigned Deputy Schmidt to Burroughs duty so I wouldn't have to leave Jenny at night. That dear little lady hasn't had anywhere near as many emergencies."

"I never minded visiting her. She gave me cookies." He cleared his throat. "I saw her and was headed home when I noticed lights in an area that should have been deserted."

"Hanging Rock?"

"You catch on fast."

One of the duties of sheriff was to do an occasional drive-by at Hanging Rock to chase away teenagers who might be using the dangerously run-down cabins for parties or for crash pads. Several times, she'd found kids sleeping under a rotted roof that might collapse at any moment.

He continued, "Though that area is uninhabited, there are several dirt roads that get close. As I approached, I saw vehicles parked along the shoulder. The scene was quiet."

"So you knew it wasn't a high school beer party."

"I killed my headlights, hid my vehicle and approached on foot. One of the vehicles parked at the side of the road was a state-patrol Crown Vic. Later I ran the plates to find out who it was. Care to guess?"

"Morrissey," she said. "Did you get other plates?"

"I did." His tone was formal. She could tell that he'd practiced this speech for courtroom presentation. "One was the DEA agent who is now in jail. Others were traced to cartel connections."

"No other cops?"

"I couldn't see all the cars," he reminded her. "There were others parked along another road. I didn't take the time to get the plates. I suspected serious business when I spotted the armed guards outside one of the cabins."

Her heart beat a little faster. Though these events had taken place over a year ago, she was scared about what he was going to find. "Armed guards?"

"Armed with semiautomatic assault weapons, similar to AK-47s."

"How can you be so calm?" She reached over and shoved his shoulder. "You should have gotten out of there."

"I'll remember that advice for the next time," he said. "I eased up close to a rear window so I could hear what was being said inside. The glass had been broken out. I was able to see over the sill. There were seven, possibly eight, men in a room where most of the drywall had been torn off the walls, leaving bare unpainted boards and wall joists. There was trash on the floor. The only light came from a battery-powered lantern on the table and from Maglites carried by some of the men. Two wooden chairs. A man sat in one and a woman in another. They both had their hands tied behind their backs. A big guy in a black leather jacket with fringe stood over them, yelling in Spanish. I could only pick up the gist of what he was saying. These two had betrayed him and cost him a lot of money. He turned toward my window. I'll never forget that face."

"Did you know him?"

"I recognized him from a BOLO Ty sent me. He was part of the Esteban cartel."

Though the APBs and BOLOs she used as scrap paper aged and dated, the danger never grew old. She had to wonder if she would have been as alert as her husband. "I only remember one from the cartel. They called him El Jefe, which is Spanish for *boss*, even though he wasn't at the very top of the leadership."

"That was the guy. El Jefe."

His ugly face had printed itself in her memory. She read danger in his cold dark eyes and sneering mouth. "You should have run."

"You might be right." As though pulling himself together, he sat up, shoved his arms into his beige cotton shirt and rolled up the sleeves. "El Jefe took out a handgun—a Glock like the one you carry—but didn't pull the trigger. He passed the gun to a DEA agent who had been working undercover in this area."

"You knew him?" she said.

"We'd met. I remembered him because he had the same initials as me—W.C., which stands for William Crowe. Not a real friendly guy. Most of the undercover agents aren't."

Sam steeled herself. She doubted she'd like the next part of what he told her, but she wanted him to think she was cool, unaffected and ready to do an ace job of investigating. Maintaining that facade, she asked another question. "Did you recognize any of the other men in the room?"

"Some faces seemed familiar. Most likely, they were cartel men I'd seen on other BOLOs. And two cops from Glenwood that you probably knew from when you worked there. One of them retired and left the area. No one has been able to reach him. The other died under suspicious circumstances."

She counted the tally. "Four men from law enforcement—two cops, Morrissey and William Crowe."

"One cop is on the run. The other and Morrissey are dead. And the DEA agent is in prison."

She swallowed hard before asking, "Why?"

"Crowe talked back to El Jefe in Spanish, said something about how this wasn't sanctioned by his boss. He handed his cell phone to Morrissey and told him, in English, to make a call. Crowe said they didn't have to do the dirty work unless their boss said so. Before Morrissey could make the call, El Jefe pointed a gun at the DEA agent. In English, he said that there were fifty thousand reasons why they should follow his orders."

He paused to take a breath and let his story sink in. She wanted to hear that the good guys in white hats rode over the hill and rescued those people, but she knew this story didn't have a happy ending.

"The woman was unconscious and slumped over," Wade said. "The man had been severely beaten and he was also pretty much out of it. Crowe aimed the Glock and pulled the trigger. He ended their suffering."

She drew the obvious conclusion. "He was arrested because of your eyewitness account."

"That's right."

His shoulders slumped, and his copper-colored gaze turned inward as though trying to see his way clear.

"You had to turn him in," she said.

"Yeah, he's guilty as hell. Yes, he murdered those people in cold blood. Dana Gregg and Lyle McFee…"

He shook his head. "They're the victims here. It's important to remember them."

"But you're still thinking about Crowe."

"I regret sending him to prison. He didn't have a choice. He was looking down the barrel of El Jefe's gun. If Crowe hadn't killed them, he would have been a dead hero. That's too much to ask."

Though he'd told this story dozens of times, the emotion seemed to touch him. In his voice, she heard an echo of the terrible helplessness he must have felt while watching a murder take place. And his remorse about pointing an accusing finger at an undercover agent in a no-win situation.

"There's nothing you could have done differently. You couldn't change what happened," she said. "Not by yourself."

"I know."

"It's not like you could call for backup. A cartel murder is way out of Deputy Schmidt's comfort zone."

"The larger problem was that I didn't know how many others from law enforcement were involved," he said. "I made the decision not to tell anyone until I talked to Ty."

His words stabbed a knife blade into her gut. *He couldn't tell anyone. Not until he talked to Ty.* What about his wife? What about her?

"Why couldn't you trust me?"

Chapter Eleven

This confrontation was painfully inevitable. Wade should have told her, should have trusted her. She was right. He was wrong.

A year ago when he'd witnessed the murders, Wade had wished that he could have come up with a reasonable excuse for why he came home very late that night, crawled into bed for a few hours and left before she was awake in the morning. But there had been nothing he could say without unraveling the whole story. To his credit, he hadn't lied to her. But he'd dodged her questions and had done everything he could to keep from having a serious conversation.

"You had every right to know," he said.

Avoiding his gaze, she sat up in the nest of sleeping bags and started getting dressed. "At first, I thought you were having an affair."

"What?" Blindsided, he stared at her. "Why?"

"Think about it, Wade. You were out late, and you were secretive about where you'd been. When I wanted to talk, you claimed to be too tired and fell into the bed. Or you came up with some other distraction. You were acting real sneaky, mister."

"Maybe."

"I should have pounced on you."

"Why didn't you?"

"Your kisses told me a different story. You didn't have the lips of a cheater. The way you held me wasn't a lie. On the night before you supposedly died, we made love and it was…" She sighed softly. Her gaze lost its sharp focus. "It was something special and hard to describe."

He remembered. "I didn't want to leave you. It was tearing me apart inside. Believe me, Samantha, if I could have told you, I would have."

"Transcendent," she said. "That night, we were more than lovers. Transcendent, we were soul mates, destined to be together—even when we were apart—for all eternity."

He was so lucky to be with this woman. More than her physical beauty, she glowed from the inside. The fact that she could still care about him, after all he'd put her through, was nothing short of a miracle.

Had he done the right thing by leaving her and going into witness protection? Faking his death? He wanted to believe that everything would turn out for the best, but he couldn't be certain.

"I couldn't tell you," he said. "Some of the blame goes to Ty. He pointed out to me that you aren't an actress or even a very good liar. If you'd known that I faked my death, you would have behaved differently."

"Understatement."

"You might even have felt like you needed to tell others, like my sister or Mrs. Burroughs or your parents."

"I might have."

She wriggled to get her jeans up to her waist and

fastened the button. Getting dressed signaled an end to their intimacy. Though he could have spent the next few hours—or maybe days or maybe forever—making love to her, they were now bound to investigate. When she pulled her long, silky, beautiful hair up into a high ponytail and twisted it into a bun, he got the message: time to switch gears.

He made one more attempt to gain her forgiveness. "I thought I was protecting you and Jenny."

"I'm aware of that theory. What you don't know won't hurt you. That works okay for a little girl like our daughter." She jammed her feet into her boots. "But I'm a grown woman. I can handle the truth."

Another apology would be too much. He could have offered a promise that he'd never lie or skirt the truth again. But he wasn't sure. Another situation might arise when the best solution involved deception.

He reached for his boots. "Anyway, that's my story. That's how it went down."

"You're not done yet. What happened after the murders?"

He wasn't proud of what he did at Hanging Rock. It would have been a hell of a lot more satisfying to brag about how he rescued the victims and rounded up the bad guys. But that wasn't what happened. Instead of being a hero, he ran away and hid.

"It was one of those times," he said, "when I was glad for my misspent youth of playing hooky and hiding in the forest. I slid back into the trees and turned invisible while the men left the old house and went to their vehicles."

"What did they do with the bodies?"

"I'm getting there," he said. "Nobody was rushing. A bunch of guys were standing in a group smoking. El

Jefe was already in his car, which happened to be one I had the license plates for. At one point, the four lawmen clustered together. I couldn't hear everything they were saying. Basically, Crowe was telling the others to keep their mouths shut."

"Trying to get away with murder," she said.

But he couldn't condemn the DEA agent for his actions. If Wade had been in a similar situation, he wasn't sure he'd have been willing to sacrifice himself for two other people who were going to get shot anyway. "Or he could have been thinking of how to get in touch with his handler. Of the four lawmen, Crowe was the only one who was supposed to be undercover."

"You're still trying to believe in him."

"I can't help feeling responsible. It's my testimony—only my testimony—that's keeping him in prison."

"Oh, please." She rolled her eyes. "I'm sure there's other evidence. When you gave them the Hanging Rock location, I assume the FBI forensics team worked their magic."

"The murder weapon was gone," he said.

"No surprise there."

"They found blood on the floor, enough to get a DNA match to the victims. The bodies had disappeared."

"And you didn't see them being moved?"

"Like I said, I couldn't keep track of everybody. It was night. Including the guards posted outside the cabin, there were twelve or so guys moving around. Cars and trucks were parked in different places. The other side of the cabin was out of my sight line. They could have thrown the bodies in the back of a truck on that side."

"Or they could still be at Hanging Rock," she said.

"The FBI made a thorough search."

"But it never hurts to take another look."

He nodded. She had read his mind.

AFTER THEY CLEANED up the sleeping bags, closed the window and left the horse barn, he sauntered toward the edge of the corral, leaned his elbows on the top of the fence and gazed toward the enclosed circle. There weren't any horses right now, but the owners would soon return for the summer, and they'd bring their three mares and two stallions.

Samantha joined him and gave his elbow a nudge. "I've been thinking. Jenny is big enough to start learning how to ride."

"I want to teach her." He'd been four when he first got on a horse at Ty's father's ranch, but there was no way he'd allow his precious daughter to go galloping off without a helmet, safety gear and proper training. "Do you really think she's ready?"

"She wants to start."

He should have known, should have been there for his daughter. His gut twisted. He felt empty inside, but not from lack of food. He craved another sort of nourishment—the fulfillment that came from being a father.

He'd missed too much of her life. A year didn't sound like long until you broke it down into weeks, hours and minutes. Every minute he was away from Jenny felt like forever. "If I had known I'd be gone as long as this, I never would have agreed to the plan. I was only supposed to be dead for two months."

"How was that going to work?"

"They arrested William Crowe and the cartel guy

I'll always think of as El Jefe. The case against these two was based on my testimony."

"It's hard to get a conviction when you don't have a body," she said. "You must have given a real convincing statement to get a judge to hold these guys."

He pointed to his jaw. "Who wouldn't believe this face?"

"Those dimples look like trouble to me."

"I wish the judge had said that, wish he'd thrown the case out of his court and set everybody free. But it wasn't really about the trial. The feds wanted to use the threat of prison to get El Jefe and Crowe to talk."

"But they didn't take the deal."

"Nope."

"They couldn't hold the prisoners indefinitely. Was there another scheduled trial?"

"They went through a bunch of legal actions. I was actually delivered to the courthouse in Austin three times."

"How long?" she asked. "How long were they going to drag this thing out?"

"Until they got what they wanted."

"Surely they have enough evidence on the cartel to start making arrests."

Proving a case against the cartel wasn't the main issue. They'd broken a ton of laws and had done so without fear of reprisal. Anybody who crossed them ended up dead. "The Esteban cartel is bulletproof. Lawbreakers tend to disappear. If they're arrested, they have access to excellent lawyers. It's amazing that they've managed to hold on to El Jefe so long. If he gets released…"

Wade's muscles tensed. If the cartel decided he was

a threat to them, the danger would be extreme. He was glad that Jenny was far away and well protected.

Similar thoughts must have been occurring to Samantha. "Are we ever going to be safe?"

"I sure as hell hope so."

"But you can't promise," she said. "And it sounds like witness protection is the only way we can escape the cartel. We'll have to start over and change our names. We'll lose our house and friends."

"That's what I was trying to avoid by faking my death."

The life they'd built in Swain County when he was sheriff had been just about perfect, and he didn't want to give it up. He'd expected to have another kid or maybe two with Samantha and to grow old together.

"You sacrificed over a year of your life, over a year of our life together. Let's make damn sure it wasn't in vain." Turning away from the corral, she dusted off her hands on her jeans, straightened the front of her denim jacket and fixed him with a steady, blue-eyed gaze. "We have to close down this smuggling operation. You and me."

Never mind that the FBI, the Colorado Bureau of Investigation and the state patrol had failed to produce viable results. Samantha was on the job. He had no logical reason to believe in her. But he did. "Any questions?"

"Fill in some blanks. What kind of smuggling are we talking about?"

"You name it. Illegal weapons, drugs, even human trafficking."

She couldn't hide the shudder that rattled her shoulders. Human trafficking was the most heinous of crimes— ripping apart families, turning young women into hookers or drug mules, forcing young men into work that could only be described as slavery. He had thought of those victims while in witness protection. His sacrifice was nothing compared to those families'.

She asked, "How does the operation work?"

"Our backyard in Swain County and a couple of other remote mountain areas are a distribution hub. Using the back roads, the cartel is able to meet with their suppliers. According to Ty, an arms deal is going down real soon. The weapons were stolen from a US Army arsenal."

"We know about the cartel," she said. "But who are the suppliers?"

"A network of dirty cops and agents from DEA and ATF who are taking payoffs and staties like Morrissey."

"Why wasn't he arrested?"

"He was questioned. Ty and his boss were trying to turn him into a snitch to get to the ringleader." He stared directly into her eyes. "That's who we're after. We need to find the ringleader."

"Is his identity a secret?"

He nodded. "The feds have been digging for almost two years, and they still don't have a name."

The ringleader arranged the deals and the distribution. He procured items to be smuggled, set up the transfer of goods and sold to the end market. His involvement touched every part of the transaction. No doubt he was paid every step of the way. And yet he remained anonymous.

"How does he pay the others?"

"It's a cash business."

"Have you looked into bank balances?"

"The FBI used their forensic accountants to check

out major suspects. They found nothing. I'd assume it's a cash business."

"Let's get started at Hanging Rock." She strode toward her SUV. "I'll drive."

He caught her wrist and turned her toward him. Her fingers climbed up his chest and laced behind his neck. For a long moment, he stood and stared at her, memorizing the pillowy fullness of her lips, the cerulean blue of her irises and the arch of her eyebrows. When they kissed, he lingered tenderly, tasting the sweet flavor of his beautiful wife. She felt so good in his arms. She felt right.

Then he took a step back. "Be careful, Samantha."

Chapter Twelve

On the drive toward Hanging Rock, Sam peered through
the windshield at thickening smoke and a cloud of dust
kicked up by the heavy-duty tires on Wade's motorcycle. He'd insisted on riding alone while she stayed in
the SUV—a precaution that made sense if he needed to
disappear quickly. He was supposed to be dead, after
all. And she agreed that they needed to choose the right
moment for him to emerge from the shadows. Following that logic, he'd chosen a route that went the long
way around to avoid well-traveled roads where he might
be seen.

She'd be glad when this charade was over. They
needed to find evidence that would nail these smugglers and make Wade's testimony irrelevant. More than
that, they needed to figure out who was running the
show—the ringleader.

While driving, she handled sheriff-type business. Her
first call was to Deputy Schmidt, who was never going
to forgive her for getting into a shoot-out yesterday and
not calling him in to help. He promised to keep people
away from the fire zone and take care of the 911 calls,
most of which were related to traffic and vehicles.

Next, she spoke to the fire marshal. Hobbs assured

her that the blaze was 90 percent contained but there were still hot spots that might flare up. He expected to have firefighters on active duty in Swain County for several more days.

Sam took a couple of deep breaths to calm herself before contacting Pansy Gardener, the main 911 operator/dispatcher. Pansy was as perceptive as a fortune-teller. Keeping a secret from her wouldn't be easy. That sweet, rosy-cheeked little woman with the fluffy bangs and the silver bun on top of her head would guess from the tone of Sam's voice that something had changed.

During the past year, Pansy had become expert in reading Sam's moods and had often sent her home with instructions to take a long bath and unclench her muscles. Sage advice, and Sam was grateful for it. If she hadn't listened to Pansy, she might have tensed into a frozen statue and then—*blam!*—shattered into a million pieces.

Last night when Sam picked up Jenny, Pansy had been suspicious, and that was before she'd really connected with Wade. All she'd done at that time was kiss him and cuff him. Now that she'd made love with her "formerly dead but not a zombie" husband, the change in her was obvious. She could feel the glow that radiated from the inside out. Her whole being was energized and bubbling with vitality. She had her passion back.

Before hitting the dispatch button on her console, Sam rubbed the corners of her mouth to erase the smile that Wade's fine loving had put there.

"Hey, Pansy, it's me."

"You sound funny. Do you have a cold?"

"It's the smoke," Sam said with a fake cough. "I'll be available today, but I might be out of touch. Most of my time will be spent with the FBI, looking into the murder of Drew Morrissey."

"I can hardly believe it," she said. "We got ourselves a real mystery in Swain County. Is that what I'm hearing in your voice? Are you excited about the investigating?"

"A man is dead. That's no reason for excitement." She wouldn't be shedding any tears for the likes of Morrissey, but surely there was someone who would grieve. "I spoke to the fire marshal and he tells me the blaze is pretty much contained."

"When did you talk to him?"

"Last night. Then again this morning."

"Well, well, well…" Pansy gave a sardonic chuckle. "I have something important to say. Let's make this a private conversation."

Immediately, Sam switched the channels on the police console. She didn't want this conversation broadcast to every other unit. "What did you want to tell me, Pansy?"

"It's the other way around," she said. "You and Justin Hobbs, eh?"

"What? Why would you think—"

"You saw him last night, and then you saw him first thing this morning. Winner, winner, chicken dinner. Congratulations, Sheriff Sam. It's about time you got some loving."

"What?"

"Don't bother denying it. I can hear that growl in your voice. You had sex."

There were a dozen ways this story could twist around and become an embarrassment. She needed to end the potential gossip right now. "There is nothing between me and Justin Hobbs."

"Whatever you say. Wink, wink."

"I swear, Pansy. He's a nice man, hardworking and a good fire marshal—"

"And big," she said. "Don't forget big. You know I love you, Sam, but you're taller than ninety percent of the men in this county. Justin is a real good fit for you. He's got to lose the beard, though."

Sam groaned. If only she could tell Pansy about Wade... "Promise you won't gossip. Tell no one."

"You got it."

"If anyone asks, I got Jenny out of town. She was having a little trouble with the smoke, and I can't skip work to take care of her, not with this murder investigation."

"It'll be good when you're married again," Pansy said. "Then you can stay home whenever you want. Not to mention the other benefits."

Wink, wink. "I'll check in later."

Wade led her farther on a dirt road that ascended through the pine forests in a loose zigzag. The usually bright scenery took on a dark, sinister quality. When she peered over the edge of the drop-off, she didn't see trees and shrubs and springtime flowers. Instead, it was a witch's cauldron of smoke. The fire marshal—who would hopefully never hear Pansy's wild accusations—had said that the blaze was under control. But that didn't mean the fire was out.

On the slope opposite her road, the devastation was severe. Charred boulders poked out from scorched earth. The towering, majestic trees had been turned to scraggly, burned matchsticks. Occasional bursts of orange skittered and died. This wasn't an active blaze, but it was still dangerous.

After a sharp right turn, Wade drove half a mile down a one-lane road, slowed his bike and stopped without dismounting. She pulled up behind him and parked. Before she left her vehicle, she put on a white ventilator mask and grabbed another for Wade.

As she approached the bike, he took off his helmet and flashed a huge grin. His dimples winked. His teeth appeared extra-white against the dirt and ash smeared across his face. Riding a motorcycle through a fire zone probably wasn't the smartest way to get from here to there.

"For the rest of the way, you're riding with me." He handed her the helmet. "Put it on."

Apparently, she was going to find out exactly how dumb it was to ride through flames. She thrust the mask at him. "This is for you."

He snapped the elastic strap that held the white mask over the nose and mouth. "Do I look like a doctor?"

"It's not a costume," she said. "It's practical."

"Wish I had an extra pair of goggles for you."

"I'll manage."

She blinked, and her memory flashed back to a time several years ago when they'd been on a motorcycle together. For a couple of days, they'd been free and wild, zooming down the highway on a big, powerful Harley-Davidson. She'd leaned her cheek against his back and wrapped her arms around him while the powerful engine vibrated between her legs. Oh yeah, she remembered very well. But that kind of memory wasn't going to help their investigation. She needed to focus.

Today was different. They were experienced, responsible, and she certainly wouldn't confuse this feisty little Honda with a Harley hog. The rugged off-road tires were impressive, but there was barely enough room for her to sit behind him. "Why can't I take the SUV? This road looks wide enough."

"The bike has better maneuverability. The SUV is safer here, farther from the fire. It gives us a second way to escape."

Escape from what? Her thoughts jumped to worst-case scenarios. A spark from the fire could turn the houses they were searching to flaming infernos. Cartel thugs armed with AK-47s might stage an assault. Leaving her trusty SUV right here was a good plan. If anything bad happened to the bike…

She plunked on the helmet, flung her leg over the seat and clamped her arms around his middle. Bouncing along on the dirt road felt like riding a bucking bronco, but she didn't care. In spite of the potential danger, being with her husband and taking charge of her life filled her with a sense of well-being.

At any moment, disaster could come crashing down on them. The consequences might be terrible. They could be injured, even killed. For now, they were partners. For now, she was happy.

Through the tree trunks and the dulling haze of smoke, she spotted the two ramshackle cabins. Both one-story structures were made of wood that had weathered to a tired gray. Both were anchored by stone fireplaces. They weren't exactly alike but similar, like first cousins. Not side by side. Nor did they face each other. They were angled, as though one cousin had insulted the other and was leaving in a huff.

Her other visits to Hanging Rock had taken place after dark, and her only reason for being there was to chase away the teenagers who might have the roof collapse on them and get hurt. She'd never taken the time to look around.

When she got off the bike and removed the helmet, she strode between the two cabins, staring at one and then the other. The house on her left was smaller and more square. The one on her right was in better shape. It had a front window that actually hadn't been broken, probably because the filth was holding it together.

A few tattered ribbons of yellow crime-scene tape decorated the less decrepit cabin. She pointed toward it. "Is that where the murders happened?"

"See for yourself." He stepped onto the porch, which was missing a few boards, and jiggled the door handle. Not locked, the door popped right open.

Inside the front room, the old floorboards were discolored in two large, irregular patches. Dried blood from the two victims. Like Wade, she wanted to know and remember their names. "The man and woman—what were their names again?"

"Dana Gregg and Lyle McFee."

"What did they do to upset El Jefe?"

"These two weren't upstanding citizens. They had long rap sheets and bad reputations. When they siphoned off a hundred thou on a drug deal, El Jefe got mad."

She gave a sniff and was glad for the mask protecting her nose. The place smelled like a foul combo of ashes from the fireplace, dried vomit, mold, feces, urine and something else she couldn't identify. "Why did the cartel use this place?"

"First rule of real estate." He snugged an arm around her waist and pulled her close as he whispered, "Location, location, location."

He pulled aside their ventilator masks for a quick but tasty kiss. Tempting, but she pushed him away. "Not here."

"Why not?"

"I can't stop thinking about all the teen sweethearts who used this place for their love nest." A particularly gross thought struck her. "You never came here, did you? When you were in high school?"

He shrugged. "Once or twice for keg parties."

"But not with a girlfriend, right?"

"Give me some credit. I may not be high class, but this?" He gestured to the rusted-out lawn chairs, graffiti on the walls and piles of rubbish. "This is just about as low as you can go."

"Whatever was I thinking? You're such a perfect gentleman."

"When you think about it," he said, "it's lucky that the cartel never bumped into the high school crowd. Ty told me that Hanging Rock was used to make exchanges. And they stored contraband here."

"Aha!" Finally, she had a starting place. "We need to make a thorough search. If they left stuff behind, there has to be a hiding place."

In a sudden move, he pinned her to the wall. Craning his neck, he looked through the open space that was once a window. He whispered, "Did you hear that?"

Keeping silent, she shook her head.

"I think somebody's out there." He pulled his Beretta from the holster and ducked so he wouldn't be seen.

There seemed to be no other choice than to draw her gun. During the year she'd been sheriff, she'd unfastened the snap on her holster only once. Since Wade's return, it was twice in as many days. She didn't like being in this position. She'd always thought that if force was necessary, a stun gun could be used. But her little zapper wasn't good for long-range shooting, and this situation required a lethal response.

The danger Wade kept talking about came closer. Following his lead, she moved carefully from one window to the next. The boards creaked under her feet. There didn't seem to be much of a wind, but the tree branches outside shifted and the shadows moved as though they'd taken on a life of their own.

Hoping to get a view from the back side of the cabin, she crept down a short hallway toward the kitchen. Disgusting! Nobody had used this room for cooking in a very long time—at least she hoped they hadn't. Part of the ceiling had collapsed. The wallpaper that hadn't been scrawled on with graffiti peeled away in strips. The sink was filth encrusted. Same with the countertops, the tiles had been pulled off to expose the bare, rotting wood. An eight-by-ten rag rug was spread carelessly over the torn green linoleum.

"Samantha," Wade called.

She dashed back into the front room in time to see him put his gun away. "What?"

Through the open front door, he showed her a family of white-tailed deer. "There are our intruders."

Relieved, she clasped her free hand over her heart. "I'm glad to see them. But I'm not."

Protecting wildlife was a passion of hers, and she knew that Wade felt the same way. She heard the emotion in his voice when he said, "When I see deer and a fire in the forest, all I can think is *Bambi*."

And he was a hunter. "Fires are an inconvenience for you and me, but for the deer and the chipmunks and raccoons and bears and moose and even the snakes, their whole world is destroyed. Their food supply is gone. The water is polluted. They have no shelter."

"Did Hobbs mention if this one was started by natural causes?"

"He hasn't said anything yet." She couldn't allow herself to get sidetracked, thinking about fire safety. Her focus needed to stay firm. "Back to business."

"Yeah, ma'am."

"When the FBI searched in this cabin for the bodies, did they find a root cellar?"

"I don't know."

Her grandma in rural Oregon had a root cellar with shelves full of canned fruit, homemade applesauce and Mason jars with pickled beets. She used to take Sam down there and show off all those racks of supplies, telling her that a well-stocked household would never go hungry.

"These cabins are in a remote area," she said. "And sometimes you can't get to a store. If there were ever people living here, they'd need a good-size pantry and root cellar."

"That's not how most of these cabins are constructed." He took her hand and led her onto the porch. After they went down two steps to solid ground, he bent over and pointed at the rocks and concrete of the foundation. "No room for a cellar."

"It doesn't even look like there's a crawl space to get under the house."

"My guess is that they slapped down rocks and cement, leveled it off and started building. It would have been easier to add a second floor than to mess with a cellar."

She remembered the struggles when they were building their own house. "I suppose you're right."

He glanced over his shoulder. "The fire is getting closer."

"That gives us a reason to get out of here fast."

"I hope the sounds I heard were only those deer." He looked toward the other cabin. "I should check around."

"Let's take a quick look in the kitchen first."

She went onto the porch, through the door and down the hallway. There was something about that rag rug on the floor that didn't seem right. Hands on hips, she stared down at it.

He pinched his nose behind the ventilator mask. "It reeks."

"The rug bothers me," she said.

"Because it doesn't go with the rest of the decor?"

"It's almost a match in terms of ugly and dirty, but not quite as tattered. Did you notice any other rugs?"

"I don't think so. Your point?"

"This rug is newer, and I'll bet somebody brought it here to use as a cover-up." She cleared the surface of the rug, moving aside the clutter, empty boxes and a wood chair with a candle melted onto the seat. With Wade's help, she peeled back the rug to reveal a floor of torn and battered linoleum.

Bending down, she checked it out. "I was really hoping we'd find something here, like a secret escape hatch."

"Our search is a long shot," he said. "I sure as hell don't think the FBI is infallible, but they're good at gathering evidence."

"Forensics is half skill, half luck and half instinct."

He squatted down beside her. "Is that something you learned at police academy?"

"The three halves are from my dad the cop." When she was a child, she used to play crime scene with her dollhouse. "Let's try one more thing. Grab the edge of that linoleum and pull it back."

"It's going to wreck the floor," he warned.

"This place is already a wreck."

Working together, they separated the ugly green flooring from the plywood below. The glue and the tacks that held the linoleum in place were long gone, so it wasn't a difficult task.

Under a large section that was flush with the wall, Sam found what she'd been looking for.

A trapdoor.

Chapter Thirteen

"Beginner's luck," Wade said as he stared down at the stained, battered plywood lid of a trapdoor.

"What does that mean?"

"On your first investigation, you've outsmarted the FBI."

He couldn't see Samantha's smile behind her ventilator mask, but she was practically wriggling out of her skin with excitement. "You don't think the FBI found the cellar?"

"I doubt they even looked. It doesn't make sense to have a cellar in this kind of cabin. You saw the rock foundation. Like you said, there's not even a crawl space."

But here he was, looking down at a trapdoor that had to lead somewhere. The thick grime crusted around the edges of the plywood door told him that it hadn't been opened recently. He thought of that night so long ago when he witnessed the murders that changed his life. Had the trapdoor been used? Was this a place where the smugglers hid their wares between transfers?

Samantha took her Maglite from a pocket in her denim jacket and waved it over the trapdoor like a magic wand. "Open sesame."

"Are you expecting me to lift it?"

"Might as well use those great big muscles of yours."

The crude trapdoor didn't have hinges, just a carved-out handhold at one end. He yanked off the lid to a small opening in the floor. When she aimed her light into the darkness, he saw a wooden ladder that looked as if it had been hammered together by a four-year-old.

"The good news," he said, "is that if the ladder breaks, there won't be far to fall. That space can't be more than six feet high."

She slanted the flashlight beam to see farther inside. "Before you go down there, you should take off your sexy leather jacket. It'll get filthy."

"What about you?"

She flipped her denim collar. "Washable."

Before descent into a smugglers' pit, only a wife would worry about getting his clothes dirty. Only Samantha would call his jacket sexy. And he agreed both ways. He liked having her fuss over him, and the fact that she considered him sexy was a definite plus.

He tossed his jacket over the back of a chair, dropped to the floor and stuck his leg down to find the first step of the ladder. With a bounce, he tested the crude rung before putting his whole weight on it. Halfway between the floor and the cellar, he paused on the ladder and sucked down a deep breath. He hated enclosed spaces. Not that he was claustrophobic. Because he was six feet five inches tall, he needed more room to spread out. At least, that was what he told himself as he forced his legs to keep going down the ladder. He stepped onto a dirt floor. A thick darkness surrounded him.

Samantha handed the Maglite down. Before flashing it in all directions, he tried to take another couple of breaths. His lungs felt pinched. The ventilator mask was smothering him. He tore it off.

She was already down the ladder. Standing in front of him, she took his chin in her hand and forced him to look directly at her. "I forgot about that thing you have with small places."

"I'm fine."

She pulled off her mask to give him a little kiss. "Let's get this done."

Taking the Maglite from him, she swept the beam across the dirt floor. Like the upstairs, there was clutter. Nothing appeared to be contraband. The space contained only discarded junk.

Neither he nor Samantha could stand upright without bumping their heads against the floor joists. The walls were dirt and cinder block. Tumbled-down shelves lined every wall of the cellar that seemed to be roughly the same size as the kitchen above it. The beam from her flashlight lingered on the pipes and plumbing fixtures that congregated in the area below the sink.

Closer to them, two black garbage bags were piled against a wall.

Samantha's fingers clamped onto his arm. Under her breath she mumbled, "Oh God oh God oh God oh God…"

Her panic made him stronger. He took the wavering Maglite from her. "This is a good thing," he said.

"Not for them."

The bags covered only part of the bodies. Legs in jeans stuck out the end. The desiccated, blackened feet were shoeless.

"Dana Gregg and Lyle McFee." Their names were a

mantra. The victims should never be forgotten. "I meant it's good that we've found the evidence."

"Does that mean the feds don't need you to testify? An eyewitness account is always helpful, but the bodies will provide the type of physical evidence that wins convictions. There will be ballistics, maybe even fingerprints." From another jacket pocket, she pulled out a pair of baby blue latex gloves. "Don't forget these."

She was right about the physical evidence being important, and it was possible that his testimony wouldn't be needed. But Samantha was forgetting the ringleader. Until the smuggling operation was dismantled, there would be danger for them and for others in Swain County.

He took the gloves and gave her a hug. "You don't have to get any closer to those bags if you don't want to."

"For a minute there, I thought I was going to throw up." She stepped away from him and waved her palm in front of her face like a fan. "I'm still flushed, but I'm mostly fine. And I want to see."

Stooped over, they moved across the uneven dirt floor, kicking clutter out of the way as they went. The distance was only a few steps, and he scanned with the light to show himself that the walls weren't really closing in. He hated being underground, hated the darkness. But he couldn't leave until he'd done what was necessary.

He wished Samantha wasn't here. The beam from the Maglite glistened on a long strand of hair that fell across her delicate cheekbone before she tucked it behind her ear. She was so lovely—gentle but strong, sexy and sweet. He wanted to protect her from the ugliness of life.

When they were standing directly over the garbage

bags, he said, "I understand that you want to be part of the investigation."

"I'm good at this, Wade. I found the cellar."

He didn't think the sight of two corpses that had been stashed in a hole for over a year was a requirement for being a good investigator. "You don't have to look. Once I tear open that bag, you can't unsee what's inside."

"If that's true, there isn't any reason for you to look, either."

With a jolt, he realized that she was correct. There was nothing about the victims that would make a difference if he saw it. Since he'd never known Dana or Lyle in real life, he couldn't identify them. And he didn't remember what they were wearing when he'd witnessed their murders. He had a vague impression of a man with a mustache and a woman with bleached-blond hair. "It's okay. I can handle this."

"But it doesn't really matter, does it?" She took a backward step and pulled him with her. "Let's get out of this dark, awful pit. I need to cool down. It's really hot in here, isn't it?"

He took his burner phone from his pocket. "I'll call Ty. His boss was supposed to be at his ranch today. We can have him meet us here and let the FBI take care of this evidence."

Like Samantha, he had become aware of the heat. A light sweat broke across his back. The stench of smoke had become nearly overwhelming.

From overhead, he heard the unmistakable sound of a footfall on the cabin floor. Not a deer. Someone had found them.

Wade looked toward the open trapdoor and saw an

orange flickering light. Fire! Before he could react, the door slammed shut.

A nightmare coming true, he couldn't believe it. They were trapped below a burning cabin with no way to escape. He should have insisted that one of them stay at the top and keep watch, should have done more to secure the area, and he should never have brought her along. No time now for recriminations and apology. He had to make this right.

A crash sounded above them. The person with the nearly silent footfalls no longer felt the need for stealth. Not a good sign.

"I can hear it," she said. "I can hear the fire crackling."

He passed her the cell phone. "Call Ty. Tell him where we are. And then you might want to call your buddy the fire marshal."

"I know what Justin Hobbs would tell me." She sounded angry, which was better than scared. He didn't want her falling apart. "He'd say that this cabin was burning too fast. It wouldn't go up like tinder. The flames need time to spread. Somebody set this blaze. Somebody did this to us."

He had come to the same conclusion. The slamming trapdoor was his first clue. "Make the calls. I'll get the trapdoor open."

There hadn't been a latch on the plywood board that served as a lid. If the wind had blown it shut, he should be able to push it back without any trouble. He climbed onto the ladder and gave a shove. The board shifted but clunked back into place. Something was on top of it, something heavy.

She was standing behind him, holding up the phone. "There's no signal."

They couldn't count on help from anywhere else. He looked up at the trapdoor. Maybe if they both pushed, they could move the board. "Switch places with me. If we work together, I think we can lift the board."

"And then what?" She pointed to the front edge of the trapdoor where the harsh light of the blaze was visible. "We'll be in the middle of a fire."

If they got the door open, would they be adding oxygen to the fire, causing it to burn harder? Were his enemies waiting outside the trapdoor to ambush him? The most obvious exit wasn't the best escape. But he had to do something.

Following his instructions, she stood on the second rung of the ladder, bracing her back against his chest. Planting his feet on the earth floor, he reached up. With his height, he ought to be able to lift the trapdoor a foot or so. When he placed the flat of his hand against the door, he discovered that the plywood surface was hot. Already on fire?

"Ready?" He prepared for a major effort. All those hours of working out might pay off. "Push now."

With their combined strength, they managed to lift the plywood a few inches. The flames licked through the opening and seared the hairs on his arms.

"Put it down," he said.

They dropped it with a thud.

She turned on the ladder and aimed the Maglite in his face. "I couldn't see much, but I'd guess the beat-up fridge in the kitchen is now on top of the trapdoor."

"That must have been the crash we heard."

"Are you okay?" she asked.

"Are you?"

She rubbed her hand up and down her sleeve. "My trusty jacket took care of me."

He tightened his arms around her. Even now, even when they were close to death, he found pleasure in her embrace. "I left my sexy leather jacket up there. By now it's toast."

"If we get out of here alive, I'll buy you another."

"And I'll wear it when I take you on our second honeymoon in Hawaii."

They had so much to live for, this couldn't be the end.

Stepping back from the crude ladder, he circled the cellar with the beam from the Maglite, searching for inspiration. He'd done a lot of the construction work on their house. This little cabin was built on a stone foundation, nothing fancy, nothing too solid. In the root cellar, the walls were cinder block and loosely cemented stone. How hard could it be to break through?

He selected a portion of wall that was away from the trapdoor and away from the sink where extra care might have been taken to keep the pipes from freezing. If his directions were accurate, they'd come out on the west side of the cabin.

Moving the first cinder block was the hardest. The wall was a flat surface with nowhere to get a grip. Avoiding the main foundation support, he reached up to the highest cinder block. He wedged his fingertips into a space between the wood floor and the block and pulled hard. He would have given a lot for some sturdy workman's gloves instead of the flimsy latex.

"What can I do?" she asked.

"Look for a shovel."

"But you need the flashlight here."

"Use the phone."

The damn thing was useless for making calls; it might as well be demoted to flashlight status. He tugged again and the cinder block moved. This plan was going to work. With a new confidence, he yanked the brick halfway out of the wall.

Wearing her ventilator mask, she returned to his side. "No shovel, but I found a tire iron."

"I'll take it."

Smoke from the fire seeped through the floorboards. He pulled up his mask but still coughed. The tire iron was the perfect tool for tearing out the cinder blocks. In minutes, he'd made a hole in the wall that they could crawl through.

He inhaled a gasp of smoke. His eyes were watering. Sweat poured down his back. The last obstacle was the cemented stone wall. It hadn't been properly maintained. Jagged cracks cut through the concrete. If he'd been in a better position, he could have knocked it down with his bare hands.

Reaching up and picking at the stones with the tire iron was slow progress. There had to be a better way. "The ladder."

"What about it?"

He was too wiped out to explain. "Bring the Maglite and come with me."

Staggering across the uneven dirt floor, he struggled to keep his focus clear. His plan was to take the crude stepladder, lift it over his head and use it as a battering ram to break through the wall. Below the trapdoor, he snatched the ladder and headed back toward his hole in the wall.

The trapdoor overhead glowed red. With the added weight of the fridge, he guessed that the plywood would collapse in seconds. The fire would be in the root cellar with them.

Wade had to move fast.

Samantha did a good job of providing support, helping when she could and staying out of the way otherwise. She seemed to instinctively know where he needed the beam of the flashlight.

He placed the ends of the ladder into the space he'd made in the cinder blocks. It was about shoulder height. Using both arms, he rammed the ladder against the stone-and-concrete wall. He muttered under his breath, "Come on, move, damn it."

Samantha held the light steady. "You're getting it. Try again."

He thrust the long wooden frame harder, again and again like a piston engine. And he felt the wall give. In only a few more strokes, he would break through.

In a burst of red embers, the trapdoor caved in. Half of the refrigerator crashed into the cellar. The fire followed. Flames leaped toward them, clawing the air and consuming the last bit of oxygen.

One more time, he slammed the ladder against the stones. This time, he felt the wall break apart. He adjusted the ladder so Samantha could climb up and push her way through the hole.

"Go," he said. "I'll follow."

She did as he said. In seconds, she was up and out. Now it was his turn. The heat from the fire seared his backside as he removed a few more stones so he could make it through the narrow space that had been an easy fit for Samantha.

He heard shots fired. Two of them.

Chapter Fourteen

Sam took aim at the neatly uniformed Lieutenant Natchez, who stood in front of her with his hands raised above his head. When she'd first spotted him lurking around in the forest, she'd shouted the standard "Police! Freeze!"

He didn't respond, and she wasn't in a patient mood. Whipping out her Glock, she'd fired two warning shots.

"My next bullet," she growled, "will be accurate."

"Knock it off, Sam. You know who I am. You can't shoot me."

Oh, but I can. Anger surged inside her, causing her pulse to race. She would have taken great pleasure in shooting off both toes on his shiny boots. What kind of jerk wore high motorcycle boots when he was driving a car?

Gritting her teeth, she tamped down her emotions and controlled herself. After the hell she'd just been through, dealing with Natchez was no big deal. In the root cellar while she was facing a terrible and almost certain death, she hadn't dissolved into tears or started wailing.

A desperate need to survive had held her together. She was different now. Controlled. Focused. Nothing was more important than closing this investigation—nothing. She hadn't got her husband back from the dead only to lose him again.

She sighted down the barrel of her Glock. "Did you set the cabin on fire?"

"Hell no."

She glanced over her shoulder at the cabin. The most intense part of the blaze was in the kitchen, which was further evidence—as if she needed more—that she and Wade had been targeted. This fire was arson.

"What are you doing here, Natchez?"

"My job," he snapped at her. "I'm doing my job, trying to find out who killed my man Morrissey."

An evasive answer if she'd ever heard one. "You've got one more chance to give me an honest answer. Why are you here? Were you following me?"

He looked down at the dirt beneath his boots and scowled. "I spotted your vehicle on the back roads and decided I should see what you were up to. Then I lost track of where you were and drove around. When I saw this fire, I figured you had something to do with it."

Looking past her shoulder, he gaped. His eyeballs popped wide open. His military-cut blond hair stood on end. He let loose with a string of curses that was amazing in its scope and variety.

She'd already guessed what he saw: Wade.

Her supposedly dead husband strode up beside her, pulling off his ventilator mask as he approached. She'd done the same. Though the air outside the cabin was hazy, it was nothing compared to the suffocating blanket of smoke in the root cellar.

"I knew it." Natchez crowed. "I knew it even before Morrissey told me. You're still alive."

Without hesitation, Wade yanked his gun from the holster and pointed it at the state patrolman. "The next time I hear you curse, I'm going to punch your teeth out. There's a lady present and she doesn't need to hear any of your bad language."

"Sure thing, Wade. You got it." His hands dropped to his sides.

"Not so fast," Wade said. "Keep your paws up."

She couldn't believe that Wade would suspect Natchez of being the clever ringleader who had outsmarted the local police and the FBI. This jerk had less intelligence than a tree frog. Oddly, his stupidity was what made her think that Natchez wasn't one of the dirty cops.

Natchez leaned toward them. "This is some kind of big-deal undercover operation. Am I right? Yeah, I am. Tell me what's going on. I want to know."

"I thought you had your hands full," she said. "You were busy doing your job, investigating Morrissey's death."

Petulant as a kid with a busted toy, he said, "Turns out I don't have jurisdiction. The feds are doing the autopsy."

"Their results?" Wade asked.

"Cause of death was two gunshot wounds to the chest. Ballistics on the bullets indicate a Colt .45 revolver."

Remembering Wade's fancy Colt with the inlaid grip that she'd removed from the car, she shuddered. All they had were ballistics. Morrissey wasn't killed in the car, so there wasn't a primary crime scene to search for clues. Not much to go on, and it all pointed to Wade. On top of everything else, he was being framed for murder.

"Your gun," she whispered in his ear.

"I know," he muttered.

"You just can't catch a break."

His beige cotton shirt was torn to shreds when he'd

crawled through the stone and cinder blocks. The exposed flesh on his chest and torso was dirty and marked with bloody scrapes. He looked as if he'd come off a battlefield. Ash and smoke made dark smears across his forehead and under his cheekbones.

She wasn't accustomed to seeing her handsome cowboy as a fierce, macho warrior, and she liked this dangerous new image. The leather jacket wasn't the only sexy thing about him.

Wade snarled at Natchez, "Have you reported this fire?"

"Not yet."

"Do it," he ordered. "Contact the fire marshal on the console in your car. And wait here for him."

According to Justin Hobbs, the fire was almost out, 90 percent contained. He wouldn't be happy to learn about renewed flames at these cabins.

"I can't waste my time waiting around," Natchez said. His lips pinched with the effort of holding back his expletives. "I got things to do."

"The FBI forensic team will be here soon," Wade said. "There's evidence for a federal case in the root cellar under the kitchen. It shouldn't be moved."

Natchez puffed out his chest. "Are you asking me to guard the evidence?"

"Yes."

Wade holstered his gun and strode toward the faithful little motorbike that stood close to the cabin that wasn't aflame. At least their transportation was still intact. She trotted along behind him.

"Hey, wait," Natchez called out. "Aren't you going to tell me how you faked your death?"

Slowly, Wade turned. He gave Natchez a cold, hostile look. "I don't have anything more to say."

She got onto the bike behind him and held on tight as they chugged down the hill to where her car was parked. The jostling of the motorcycle should have kept her adrenaline pumping, but when she leaned her cheek against his back, she felt herself beginning to relax. She was tired. Not even noon, and she was already tired. How was she going to make it through the rest of the day?

"I've got an idea," she said. "Hide the motorcycle and ride in the car with me. We could go back to the house and get cleaned up."

"We can't quit now. We're making progress."

She wasn't seeing the same picture that he was. "How do you figure?"

"We found the bodies. That was your smart thinking."

Yes, indeed, she'd used some sharp observation and clever logic. Because of him, they had been in the right place at the right time. They worked well together. Though she'd like to spend more time developing intimacy, she had two bodies to deal with. And she needed to catch the person who set the cabin on fire and tried to trap them inside.

He guided the motorcycle to a stop behind her SUV.

"I'm keeping the bike," he said. "I might need it."

She dismounted and took off the helmet. Her ventilator mask hung by the elastic strap around her neck, but she didn't put it on. With a sigh, she adjusted her focus and turned the dial back to investigating.

"Natchez," she said. "He turned up at the very moment when we got attacked. Seems like too much of a coincidence."

He shut off the engine on the motorcycle, got off and paced along the road, stretching his shoulders and back. "I wouldn't be surprised if Natchez was part of the smuggling operation. Those state-patrol guys have a lot of autonomy. He could cruise anywhere in Colorado in his Crown Vic, and nobody would question his right to be there."

"Which would make it easy for him to facilitate the smuggling."

"Making sure the goods got from point A to point B."

She nodded. It was easy to imagine Natchez meeting schedules and bossing other people around. He was a middle-management type, a lieutenant who would never become captain. "He's the sort of guy who follows orders."

"But not the boss," Wade said, "not the ringleader."

"Why was he following me? Someone must have given that order. But why?"

"Because of me." He stopped pacing and leaned against her SUV. "He said that Morrissey told him I was still alive. If a snitch like Morrissey knows, the word is out. Natchez was watching you in the hope that you'd lead him to me."

So far, she was following everything he said. "Did Natchez start the fire and trap us in the cellar?"

"That's a negative." His smile activated dimples on both sides of his mouth. "His uniform was spotless. No way had he been playing with fire and pushing refrigerators across the grungy linoleum."

"But maybe he saw who did it."

"I hadn't thought of that." He pushed away from her SUV. "We might need to lean harder on Natchez and get him to talk."

"What are we doing now?"

"We need to go to the Baxter ranch to see Ty and his boss, Everett Hurtado. I'll meet you there."

As he stepped around her, their hands touched. Their fingers linked. In this small way, they joined together.

Investigating together was something new. Their connection as a married couple had grown from an intense love and trust. They'd shared the experience of birthing a baby, of raising her and of watching her grow. Before Wade faked his death, Sam had believed there was nothing stronger than their relationship. Not anymore. They were working together, thinking with one mind.

Their relationship wasn't perfect, not by a long shot. There were cracks in their perfect bond. She didn't trust him implicitly. She had doubts.

She lifted their linked fingers and kissed the scarred skin on his knuckles. He was trying so hard to make everything right, but when she looked into his light brown eyes, she didn't lose herself in his gaze.

"Back there, in the root cellar," she said, "I had a really bad feeling. I was scared that we might not make it out alive. I thought about Jenny. It would be so hard for her."

He dropped a light kiss on her forehead. "It was hard for you. When I was supposedly dead, it had to be hard."

"I thought about that. In the cellar when the fire was coming closer, I tried to imagine if it would be worse to lose you again or to die together."

"I vote no on both options," he said.

So did she, but the dark thoughts about possible future disasters were still there. Before he disappeared and supposedly died, she was a happily-ever-after type of woman who preferred to live on the sunny side of the mountain. Tragedy had forced her to look at the shadows. After all those nights when she was sleeping alone, aching for the company of a good strong man, she was left with a bone-deep chill. It was going to take a while to warm up.

She stepped away from him. "See you at the Baxters' place."

"Do you have any extra windbreakers in the back?" He plucked at the tattered sleeve of his shirt. "I look like a scarecrow."

"You might be in luck." She went around the SUV and unlocked the rear. "As you well know, the annual budget for the sheriff's department is pitiful. But I had several of the extra-extra-large windbreakers left over from when you were the big boss man, literally."

He dug into a duffel bag and pulled out a navy blue windbreaker with *Sheriff* stenciled across the back. Though the jacket was wrinkled, it was an improvement over the ragged shirt.

From inside her jacket, Sam heard the "Let It Go" ringtone for Jenny. A twinge of worry went through her as she walked around to the front of the SUV to answer.

The voice on the other end was her mother. "Sam, we have a problem."

Chapter Fifteen

The arrangements she'd made with her parents to take Jenny out of town was the one thing Sam thought she'd done right. She'd got her daughter away from possible danger. And now her mom was calling about a problem.

Clenching her jaw tightly, Sam asked, "What's wrong, Mom? Was there something I forgot to pack?"

"It's the Cessna, the *Lucky Lindstrom*. We ran into some mechanical problems outside Salt Lake City and—"

"Are you all right? Is Jenny all right?" Panic shot through Sam. A plane crash?

"There was never any danger," her mom said. "We're all fine. Well, your dad is grumpy but that's just him."

Sam's panic lessened. "Let me start over. Is something wrong?"

"Well, we had to land at this strange little airfield in the middle of nowhere. Not really nowhere. It's Utah and the landscape is pretty doggone gorgeous. You've got your snowcapped mountain peaks and your interesting rock formations. Lots of cows—you call them cattle, right?"

While her mother talked, Sam's tension ratcheted up a few notches. Cora Lindstrom was known for her ability to chat endlessly. Sam might be standing here for hours if she didn't move things along. "Long story short, Mom."

"We're renting a car and driving back to Colorado."

Hysteria screamed inside her head. Sam couldn't think, couldn't reason. They couldn't come back. That wasn't according to plan. "Let me talk to Jenny."

It took only a second before Sam heard, "Hi, Mommy." The sound of her daughter's voice had a calming effect. "Grandpa is unhappy about his little airplane, and Grandma says he ought to get rid of it."

"It looks like you won't get all the way to the beach in Oregon."

"It's okay," she said. "Grandma brought Poppy the puppy on the airplane. When Poppy comes to Colorado, we have to watch her or she'll get lost in the woods."

Sam felt her breathing return to normal. "I love you, kiddo."

"Love you back."

"Put Grandma on the phone."

Explaining the situation to her mother was going to be difficult. She couldn't tell her that Wade was alive because Cora would then want to tell Jenny. But if Sam didn't tell her mom what happened to Wade, the threat from the drug cartel and dirty cops didn't make any sense.

She had to convince her parents to go somewhere else, to take Jenny and stay away from Swain County. The threat was real. Less than an hour ago, she and Wade had been close to death. She had to keep Jenny safe.

Sam's mind was blank.

After stumbling through a bit more conversation with

her mom, Sam made an excuse to get off the phone. Later, she might come up with a believable explanation that wasn't all smoke and mirrors. She refused to take the same lying path that Wade had followed. But how could she tell the truth?

She disconnected the call, stomped around her vehicle and glared at her husband, who was sitting on the back catching his breath. This was his fault. One lie led to another and another.

"Problem?" he asked.

"That was my mom."

"Is Jenny okay?"

"She's fine." She waved goodbye to him. The last thing she wanted was input from him. "Later."

While she drove on back roads toward the Baxter ranch, Sam tried to figure out what to do about Jenny. As long as her parents kept their distance, her daughter was safe. If they got too close to Swain County, the ringleader might decide that the way to get to Wade would be through Jenny.

Wade's survival seemed to be breaking news. Natchez said that Morrissey had told him. Who told Morrissey? Was the person who told him the same person who killed him?

Whoever murdered Morrissey had used Wade's gun to do the job. Life would have been easier if Sam had found fingerprints when she dusted the Colt. That weapon was spotless. She'd even checked the bullets and found nothing. It was no surprise that the gun was clean. Wade had been fairly sure that the ringleader was in law enforcement, and cops knew better than to leave prints.

On the final approach to the Baxter ranch, she took off her denim jacket. She'd left early in the morning when it was chilly, layering up with a white tank top and a blue-striped cotton shirt. She unbuttoned the front of the shirt and untucked the tail to let it hang down to cover her holster. Not that anybody would be surprised to see Sheriff Sam with a weapon strapped to her hip.

Maybe because of her five-pointed, tin-star badge, people expected her to be strong, cool and self-controlled. Most of the time, she expected that from herself. Not right now.

She stood on a precipice of tears, paralyzed and staring down into the abyss, unable to decide what she should do. She wanted to point her SUV west and keep driving until she found Jenny and could carry her away to safety. But she also needed to be here with Wade and complete the investigation so he could rejoin their family.

If only he'd talked to her before he came up with the ridiculous plan to fake his death, things would be different. She would never have allowed this charade to play out for more than a year. She would have got results… or died trying.

A sane voice in her head reminded her that she knew very little about this sort of investigation. She didn't live in a world where each decision might make the difference between life and death. If she'd been involved from the start, she might have already been a casualty.

Making a right, she drove her SUV through the gate and down the long asphalt driveway that arrowed toward the front door of the two-story main house. The Baxter ranch had been in business since a few years after World War II and was the largest cattle-raising operation in the county. The herd ranged from five to ten thousand, depending on finance and marketing. Sam had heard they'd cut back on the number of cattle while they were in a transition period. Ty's older brother, Logan, was taking over the major operations from their dad. He and his wife lived in the main house with Mama and Papa. Mama Baxter, Maggie, was one of the kindest women Sam had ever known. Also, one of the most hardworking; she never took a break.

Sam found a place to park her SUV near one of the outbuildings. As she headed toward the main house, she saw Wade standing on the wraparound front porch talking to Maggie Baxter. Actually, he wasn't doing much talking. Mama was giving a serious lecture. With both fists planted on her round hips, she glared at Wade through her wire-rimmed glasses.

As Sam came closer, she caught a taste of what Mama was saying to Wade, starting with how faking his death was the dumbest thing she'd ever heard and ending with how he'd broken the hearts of his friends and his dear, wonderful family. *Thank you, Maggie.*

Though she hated to interrupt the tirade, Sam made some noise with her boot heels when she climbed the steps onto the porch. Mama came toward her with arms outstretched. She was a sturdy woman but only about five feet tall. When Sam embraced her, she had to bend over.

Mama was crying. "Isn't it wonderful? Wade didn't die after all."

She looked over Mama's head to where her husband stood with his shoulders slumped and a look of shame and misery on his face. Sam really hoped he was aware of the sincere grief he'd caused this good, kind woman.

Mama lifted her tearstained face, looked up at Sam and said, "I could just kill that inconsiderate butthead.

Who does he think he is? Pulling a stunt like that? I should turn him over my knee like I did when he was a kid."

She'd spoken loudly enough to be sure Wade heard. In case he hadn't been paying attention, she repeated, "Inconsiderate butthead."

He took a step toward them. "I'm sorry, Maggie."

"I know you are." She patted his cheek. Her mouth drew into a bow as though she wanted to give him a kiss. But she didn't, and she didn't accept his apology, either.

He edged past them on his way to the front door. "I need to clean up before Ty's boss gets here."

"Upstairs bathroom."

"Can I borrow some clothes?"

"Ty keeps some things in the middle bedroom—the one with the bucking-bronco wallpaper. They ought to fit. Help yourself."

"Thanks." His gaze flicked back and forth between them. "Once again, I'm sorry."

He disappeared into the house.

With her thumb, Sam wiped the tears from Mama's cheeks. "You never really spanked those boys, did you?"

"Corporal punishment wasn't much of an option. In fifth grade they were as tall as I am. The threat was enough." She took Sam's arm and bustled toward the door. "Come on inside and have some lemonade. How are you feeling about all this?"

"Pretty much the same as you," she said. "Mad as hell about being lied to. But incredibly happy that he's alive."

In the huge kitchen where meals were prepared for the ranch hands and family, Mama had a young woman from town helping out. Sam knew her, and they exchanged greetings while she went to the refrigerator for a bottled water. Mama poured them each an ice-cold glass of lemonade, which she placed on the kitchen table along with a plateful of snickerdoodle cookies.

As soon as she sat at the table, Sam finished off half the water with one long glug.

"I guess you're thirsty," Mama said.

"Being nearly burned alive has that effect."

Mama and her kitchen helper both plunked down at the table. "Tell us all about it."

Sam knew it went against protocol to talk to civilians about an ongoing investigation, and she would steer clear of actual information or evidence, like finding the dead bodies or possible suspects. But she really wanted someone else's opinion on what was happening between her and Wade.

Taking a bite of snickerdoodle, she started talking about being "trapped" inside one of the cabins near Hanging Rock. There was no need to embellish the horror she'd experienced in the root cellar. The truth was bad enough.

"Were you scared?" Mama asked. "Never mind— that was a dumb question. Of course you were scared. Why did you do it?"

"What do you mean?" Sam asked.

"Why did you go looking for evidence with Wade?"

"The last time he got involved in this investigation, he deceived me and disappeared for over a year. If I had been involved, that never would have happened. From now on I want to work with him."

Mama Baxter gently placed her hand atop Sam's. Behind her glasses, her blue eyes were leaking again. "You could have both been killed. Your little girl would have had to grow up without a mother or father."

"And that's why I can't be too angry with Wade. He didn't tell me the truth because he was trying to protect us."

And now she was trying to protect Jenny. It occurred to her that Maggie's feelings and opinions were a mirror image of her own. She might be the best person to talk to about how to handle her parents about bringing Jenny back to Colorado.

Ty and Logan rolled through the back door into the kitchen, laughing and poking at each other like a couple of schoolboys. The two brothers were tall and lean, but the resemblance ended there. Logan's hair was an uncombed mass of blond curls. He had a big sloppy grin and his nose had been broken more than once. When he greeted Sam, he lifted her out of her chair in a hug and swatted her behind. Ty would never do such a thing. His brown hair was neat to match his handsome features and his attitude. The FBI was a good calling for him. Both men kissed their mother and grabbed cookies.

Ty checked a message on his cell phone. "My boss will be here real soon. I told him to land in front so he won't spook the horses in the corral."

"The horses will be fine," his mother said.

"Yeah," Logan chimed in. "Your boss isn't the only person who comes here in a chopper."

"Sorry for trying to be considerate."

Sam hadn't seen Ty since yesterday, and she had questions about the guys who attacked them. Ty had gone to the hospital with them and might have information. Plus, he'd know about the FBI forensics on the car where they found Morrissey's body.

She cleared her throat. "Before your boss gets here, you and I should talk."

"Why is that?"

Did she really have to tell him? "I need to be aware of the evidence you've obtained on the murder and the men who ambushed us."

"But I already talked to Wade."

"But I'm the sheriff," she said.

"I talked to your husband."

The three women fired hostile glares so powerful that he took a backward step. Ty got it. He backed down as fast as he could.

"I didn't mean that the way it sounded, Sam. I swear I didn't. Ask me anything. I can't hand over my official FBI report, but I can show it to you on my computer."

Though it hadn't been her intention to put him on the spot, Sam took advantage of the situation. "There's something else I've wanted to ask ever since Wade came back."

"Go ahead. Shoot."

"What really happened on the day you and your boss and my husband got together and faked his death?"

Chapter Sixteen

The moment Wade strode into the kitchen, Sam felt a change in the energy. There was something strong and vital about him, something the two Baxter men lacked. And her husband was number one when it came to handsome. In her opinion, he was almost too gorgeous with the dimples and the deep-set eyes and the chiseled cheekbones. His brown hair was wet and spiky from the shower. The smears of cellar dirt, ash and blood had been erased, and there was an aura of freshness about him as he finished buttoning a clean flannel shirt.

Though she was fairly sure that her heart was jumping out of her chest, Sam squashed the mad attraction that she felt for the man she'd married. She needed to make adjustments in their relationship. She had to learn to trust him again.

"I should be the one to tell this story," he said.

"What story?" Sam had already forgotten what she'd asked.

"About that day," he said. "The day when I didn't die in the river."

She gave a nod and leaned back in her chair at the kitchen table. Every eye in the room focused on him. Even the woman who was helping Mama with the cooking had stopped chopping and stirring to stare. Wade had that effect on people. He was compelling, a natural-born leader. But trustworthy?

"I remember every damn detail," he said. "The way the sun flashed on the river rapids, a granite ledge where some fool painted his initials in green, the frigid cold of the water, everything. I remember the hum the tires made on the highway and the crunch when we drove on gravel. I heard the echo of a bird song."

Logan asked, "Why do you remember so much?"

"It was the worst day of my life. My feet were heavy as bricks. I could barely lift them because I was sure, one hundred percent sure, that I was walking in the wrong direction."

She couldn't avoid being sympathetic toward him, but she had a very different perspective. Sure, he felt guilty for deceiving her. But she had to live with that deception, to plan his funeral, to file insurance claims, to give away his clothes. Either way, it was painful.

"I'll start at the beginning," Wade said. "At nine o'clock in the morning, Ty picked me up at the house. I kissed Samantha and Jenny goodbye."

She remembered, too. At dawn's first light, they'd made love before Jenny was up and demanding breakfast. Their morning sex was the fourth time in less than twenty-four hours. Not unheard of for them, but a little overly energetic for a married couple with a four-year-old.

At any time in those twenty-four, very intimate hours, he could have told her what was going on. He could have changed the plan. But he didn't.

"I packed all the stuff I'd need to go hunting. I had a new, handcrafted reflex bow I wanted to test," he said.

"Our cover story was that Ty and me were taking his boss and another fed out in the woods for the day. In the days before, we had plotted our route. It wasn't easy to find a spot near the white-water rapids that was feasible for bow hunting."

"I used a couple of GPS computer programs," Ty put in. "We had to make it believable that Wade could have been swept away in the current and his body never found."

It was obvious to her that Ty wasn't as emotionally invested in their story. His voice was calm, almost callous. If the shoe had been on the other foot, Ty's foot, would he have been so laid-back?

"The kayakers," Wade said, "were two federal agents from the navy. We borrowed them from their headquarters in San Diego. They were in great shape and expert in kayaking. When we got to the site on the river, they acted out what might happen if one of them lost control and I jumped in to save him."

"Would you?" she asked. "If the kayaker had really been in trouble, would you have tried to rescue him?"

"I don't know. It took a long time to figure out how it would have been possible for me to be in a position to help."

"That didn't stop you from wanting a demonstration," Ty said. "I couldn't believe you. Being thorough is one thing. You were obsessive about how the rescue attempt would have worked. You even got your ass in that freezing water."

"So did the guys from San Diego," Wade said.

"They were wearing wet suits." Ty jabbed an accusing finger in Wade's direction. "You had me worried, buddy. You weren't acting entirely rational."

"Hey, you and your boss were the ones who thought I should die. It wasn't my first choice."

"You're not blaming this on me," Ty said. "You could have backed out at any time, but you didn't. And you went a little crazy. Remember what you did to your bow. That was a beautiful piece of equipment, and you smashed it all to hell."

When they'd brought Wade's personal effects to her, the pieces of his hunting bow had broken her heart. "It was black walnut and maple. You loved that thing."

Wade shrugged. "Ty's right. I snapped."

"We were talking about how injured the kayaker ought to be," Ty said. "And trying to get a clear picture of how Wade could get in the water. Would he lose his backpack? How far along the river would he go before he got sucked under?"

The picture he was painting had become a little too vivid. Sam summarized what happened next. "You boys acted it out, and Wade went into custody as a protected witness."

"I got into the back of a van. The federal marshals were driving. They told me to lie on the bench until we were a good distance out of Colorado."

"They must have done that because they were taking you on the highway," she said. There were many traffic cameras along the main highway routes. The lenses shouldn't be able to see into the rear of a van, but it was better not to take chances.

"All the way to Texas. I must have gotten out of the van and gone inside, but I don't remember. Several days blurred together. All I could think about was you and Jenny. I missed you so much it hurt."

Sam believed him. His eyes were sad. The lines

in his face seemed to be more deeply etched. But she hadn't forgotten what happened to her when he went missing.

"Should I tell you more about what happened at the river?" Ty asked.

Sam had been kept away from the search and the investigation. "I want to know."

"My boss and I talked to the sheriff's office in Pitkin County, the Colorado Bureau of Investigation and the state patrol. Here's a twist for you. I think Morrissey took our statements. Search-and-rescue teams were deployed to locate Wade's remains."

Ty's mother interrupted. "I always thought it was strange that they couldn't find Wade. Every couple of years, the river claims a victim. But the bodies usually turn up."

"It helped," Ty said, "that we were in law enforcement. The local cops accepted our statements without question. There was nothing suspicious about it. Everybody saw this as a tragedy."

"Including me," Sam said in a small voice.

The river accident made for high drama as the kayakers, the cops and the searchers frantically attempted the rescue of a man they all liked and respected. The moment when she'd been told was far different.

Since Ty was busy at the scene, the task of notification should have gone to Deputy Caleb Schmidt or one of the others. But Maggie knew better, and she took charge. As soon as Ty called his mother, she grabbed Tyler's wife, Loretta, and the twins, who were staying at the ranch. They all went to Sam's house.

When Sam opened the door and saw the tear tracks on Maggie's cheeks and matching sorrow from Loretta, she knew something terrible had happened. Maggie didn't say a word until she'd shooed Sam into the kitchen to make a fresh pot of coffee and sent Jenny back to the ranch with Loretta and the twins. Then she sat down with Sam.

Quietly, she had received the news that her husband was dead.

Thinking of that moment turned Sam's blood to ice water. She'd felt empty. The air had left her lungs. The strength had vanished from her muscles. She hadn't been able to stand or move.

She remembered reaching for her coffee mug. Her arm seemed disconnected from the rest of her body, as though it was someone else's arm. Her hand fell limply to her lap. Her head weighed a thousand pounds, and her neck wasn't strong enough to hold it up. She drooped forward in her chair. Before she passed out, Maggie grabbed her shoulders and gave them a shake.

Maggie's lips moved. She must have said something, but Sam couldn't comprehend the words. Every woman who married a lawman—even a sheriff in a rural Colorado county—had to prepare herself for the possibility that her husband might not survive his shift.

Her mom, Cora, knew the drill and had advised her daughter to make sure their wills were properly updated, life-insurance policies were paid up and monetary accounts were in either his or her name.

When she looked around the kitchen table at the Baxter ranch, she realized everyone was watching her. They were concerned, and she appreciated their kindness. But there were some things she couldn't explain.

"I grew up knowing what to do," she said. "My mom taught me. When a cop, like my dad, dies, you've got to take care of business. Wade and I had discussed everything. We both wanted to be cremated and to have the ashes spread from the highest point on our property. There was only one problem with that." She looked over at him. "No ashes."

He winced. "It feels like I should say I'm sorry."

"Not necessary." She rose from the chair and stepped into his embrace. "Having you back is a dream come true. I must have imagined it a million times. In the first months after your fake death, I kept thinking I saw you on the street or driving past in a car. You didn't do any of those things, did you?"

"I wanted to," he admitted. "My handlers wouldn't let me. They take the witness-protection thing real seriously."

"It damn well better be serious." None of this was a joke. Her life had been shredded for the sake of this investigation. "I used to go down to the Roaring Fork, where the kayak accident supposedly took place, and stand and stare at the water. I never got you a gravestone."

"That's a mighty good thing." Maggie rose from her chair. Though she was by far the oldest person in the room, her ears must have been the sharpest. She cocked her head and pointed skyward. "I hear your boss's chopper, Ty."

Arm in arm with her husband, Sam walked toward the front porch with the others. The midsize helicopter angled around and made a landing near the fence at the edge of the road. The whirring blades churned up the dust and blew the hair back from her face.

It was an impressive entrance…and an expensive one. She hated to think of how her meager sheriff's budget compared with the vast resources of the FBI. Swain County could barely afford to buy disposable ventilation masks to use in a wildfire. Keeping her husband away from her for more than a year with a couple of marshals guarding him must have cost a pretty penny. If they didn't shut down the smuggling operations and put the ringleader out of business, that money would have been wasted.

Everett Hurtado disembarked from the FBI chopper and strode toward the ranch house. In his black suit and blue shirt with a silver-striped tie flapping in the wind from the rotors, he projected an authority figure. She didn't like him.

The first time she'd met the slender man with cold obsidian eyes and black hair was a few hours after Maggie came to her house to tell her about the accident. Hurtado had accompanied Ty. His intention was to pay his respects, but she'd sensed something phony about him. Big surprise! The whole accident and death were phony. But she hadn't got the same feeling from Ty. He radiated guilt and also sympathy, knowing how hard the faked death would be on her.

Watching Hurtado approach with two other agents trailing in his wake, she made a decision. She didn't want to be part of whatever planning session they were going to have. In a closed room with all those guys, she'd have to shout to make her voice heard, and she wasn't in the mood for that kind of struggle. She knew what she needed. Her agenda was clear: investigate with Wade and keep her daughter safe.

The decision about how to handle her mom was still dangling over her head. Sam knew the best person to give her advice on that topic was Maggie Baxter.

She gave Wade's arm a squeeze and looked up at him. "Don't go anywhere, and I mean don't leave this house, without telling me."

"Aren't you going to wait around and say hello?"

"I'd rather get cleaned up."

She didn't offer further explanation.

Wade had told her that the ringleader—the man who coordinated with the cartel and facilitated the exchange of merchandise—was someone in law enforcement. In her mind, Everett Hurtado's name belonged on that list.

For that matter, it could also be Ty.

Wade leaned down to whisper, "That call from your mom. What was it about?"

"We can talk about it later."

They used to discuss everything. His opinion was important to her. Now she was reluctant. Her love for him was undeniable, but she didn't want to confide in him. She still didn't trust him.

Chapter Seventeen

Ty escorted Wade and his boss and two other agents who were eerily similar in appearance into the front office used by his father. From what Wade had gathered, most of the real work of the ranch was being done by Logan and the ranch manager while Papa eased into retirement. The desk in Papa Baxter's office was tidy and pristine. His computer had a light coat of dust and looked as if it was seldom used, which was probably accurate. The old man liked the things that computers could do, but he had a hard time typing. Like a lot of cowboys, his hands were calloused and beat up.

The five of them could have fit comfortably in a conversational area that had a sofa and padded leather chairs, but Hurtado opted for the throne-like seat behind the big desk. The other three men worked for him. Wade didn't; he had the luxury of not following orders.

Instead of hunching around the desk, he took one of the leather chairs and stretched his long legs out in front of him.

He wished that Samantha was here with him, but he completely understood why she'd gone off in another direction. He hated briefings almost as much as she did.

If there hadn't been so much information the FBI had that he wanted, he would have left.

"Gentlemen," said Hurtado, "we'll start with the good news. Wade?"

He sounded as if he was taking roll call. "What?"

"I have a hospital report. You'll be happy to hear that neither of the survivors from yesterday's shoot-out mentioned seeing you. Their stories are consistent—full of lies but consistent. Both are expected to make a full recovery."

He hadn't killed anybody. Actually, he considered that to be very good news. Wade had never been the sort of lawman who wanted a high body count. The fewer people injured the better. "Have they been identified?"

Hurtado gestured to his matching set of agents. One of them rifled through a briefcase that contained several file folders. His twin agent whipped out a small computer, fired it up and started scrolling. The competing technologies were interesting, and Wade found himself silently rooting for the guy with the briefcase. Even more interesting was Hurtado, sitting behind the big desk with an attitude of smug superiority. There was so much about this guy that Wade disliked. How did he let Hurtado talk him into witness protection?

The briefcase won the race. He rattled off names of the survivors and the third man who had died. The names meant nothing to Wade.

When he looked at the photographs the briefcase guy handed to him, he felt a jolt of recognition. "I've seen him before. Right before the most recent start to the trial, he was at the federal courthouse in Austin. Do you have an address for him?"

Ty picked up the photo and gave it a hard look. "I'm

pretty sure I don't know him. Are you thinking he might be a local?"

"I've seen him around and about." His brain couldn't fill in that last blank. "In Austin, I knew he looked familiar."

"That's what got you spooked," Hurtado said. "You thought this guy recognized you. And you assumed that he would report back to his superiors that Wade Calloway wasn't dead."

"And my family would be in danger."

"If you had told us—"

"But I didn't," Wade interrupted. "Could we move this along? I have a couple of questions."

"Next point of discussion," Hurtado said. "That would be the murder of state patrolman Drew Morrissey. I should tell you right now that Morrissey was my snitch."

Wade had suspected as much. When he'd witnessed the murders, he'd identified some of the cops in the room. The next logical move for SSA Hurtado would be to find a contact, like Morrissey, and offer him a deal in exchange for informing on the others.

While Hurtado bragged about his communications with his snitch, Wade wondered how he could have talked to a supposed insider for over a year and yet failed to learn the name of the ringleader. Either Morrissey was so low on the totem pole that he couldn't see the top or he was playing Hurtado.

The briefcase guy spread photographs across the desktop while Hurtado explained, "These are the pictures taken by Wade's wife before she attempted to move the body."

Wade straightened in his chair. "Samantha Calloway is Swain County sheriff. She's been duly elected to that position, and that's how you should refer to her."

"I recommend not making her angry," Ty said.

One of the twin agents snickered. "Are you scared of her?"

"Damn right," Ty said, "and you should be, too."

"It was quick thinking on Sheriff Calloway's part that got us these photos," Hurtado said. "She didn't have a crime-scene processing kit and made do with her camera phone and emailed the photos to Ty's phone, and then he sent them on to me. As you can see from the pictures, it's obvious from the lack of blood spatter that Morrissey was *not* killed in this vehicle."

This was old news for Wade. "Do you have any clue about the primary murder scene? Has anybody checked out his home? Or the last place he was seen alive?"

"Good questions," Hurtado said. "We've been to his apartment. The bed doesn't appear to have been slept in. A canvass of the neighbors indicated that no one saw him last night."

Maybe he'd been killed the night before. "What was TOD from the autopsy?"

"Time of death was between ten in the morning and noon. His last meal was bacon and eggs."

"That doesn't help much," Ty said. "He could have had breakfast anywhere."

Hurtado stood behind the desk, supposedly to shuffle the array of photos. Wade thought the real reason he was standing was to be able to look each of them in the eye and assert his authority.

"I deeply regret Morrissey's death," Hurtado said with gravity. "I blame myself."

"You think somebody found out he was a snitch?" Wade asked.

"Why else would he be killed?"

Off the top of his head, Wade could think of a dozen reasons, starting with Morrissey was an irritating jerk. He was lazy, always trying to figure out a way to get out of paperwork. But he was quick to grab credit when he worked with the deputies in Swain County. "He was a pig."

"Excuse me." Hurtado lifted an eyebrow. Like his hair, his brows were very black.

"He came to a barbecue at my house," Wade said. "I hadn't really planned to invite him, but there he was. He ate enough for three people and slopped sauce all over himself."

Thinking back, Wade recalled that night, a casual get-together of men and women mostly from the community and from local law enforcement. Natchez had been there; he had to drive Morrissey home after he'd had too much to drink. Wade remembered talking to both of them about custom-made weaponry. He'd just got his black-walnut-and-maple bow and led a group into his study, where he unlocked the weapons case. His Colt .45 with the fancy copper inlay on the grip had been in there. Morrissey had commented on it.

Had he been the one who'd stolen the gun from the house? But why? It didn't make sense for him to steal the weapon that was used to kill him.

As if reading his mind, Hurtado said, "The autopsy gave us some interesting data to work with. Ballistics indicate that the murder weapon was a Colt .45 revolver. There aren't many of those antiques still around."

Ty shot him a glance. "Didn't you have one of those?"

"Still do. A collector's piece with copper inlay on the grip, it's locked in my gun cabinet at home."

He lied without hesitation. The gun had been wiped clean of prints and was, therefore, useless as viable evidence. If they figured out who had gone to the trouble of stealing the gun and planting it, they'd probably be looking at the murderer. Who would go to so much trouble to implicate Wade in the crime? It had to be somebody who knew he wasn't dead. Otherwise, why frame him?

His gaze lingered on Hurtado. At best, he was annoying. At worst…a murderer?

Wade left the comfortable chair and stalked toward the desk. His suspicions were out of hand. Or were they? Hurtado wouldn't be the first FBI agent to go rogue. "I have a question."

Hurtado shuffled impatiently through the photos. "I'd rather stick to my agenda. There's an order to be followed. I want to make sure we don't miss anything."

A spurt of righteous anger prompted Wade to say, "Yeah, you wouldn't want to overlook something important, like the bodies of Dana Gregg and Lyle McFee."

"Who?"

"The victims. The two people whose murders I witnessed. At least show them the respect of recalling their names. Dana Gregg. Lyle McFee."

"Don't lecture me on victimology."

Wade didn't think he was using the term correctly. And he didn't care for labels anyway. "This isn't about your policy for vics or perps or anybody else. It's about human decency. These two people made mistakes in their lives. They weren't saints, but that doesn't mean they deserved to be murdered. It's our job to find justice for them."

Usually, he wasn't one for big declarations, but sometimes it was important to speak out. Hurtado used the FBI to build up his own power and status. He liked swooping around in helicopters, wearing sharp suits and giving the guys who worked under him a hard time. He'd forgotten that the job was about protecting those who couldn't help themselves.

He focused his black-eyed gaze on Wade. He was angry. His features were set in granite, and his lips barely moved when he said, "Are you done with your tantrum?"

"Not really," Wade said in an aggressively cheery tone. "Have your forensic guys drawn any conclusions from the evidence we uncovered at Hanging Rock?"

"Nothing yet," he snapped.

Wade couldn't resist another dig. "I wonder why they didn't find the root cellar the first time they went looking."

"At least they didn't burn the building down."

"Neither did we," Wade said. "It was arson."

Hurtado's stony mask twitched into a frown, and Wade took that as a sign. The SSA was weakening. He knew he was in the wrong. "Fire Marshal Hobbs says it was arson. A fire with accelerant started in the kitchen. By the way, he's not happy with you."

"He'll have to stand in line before he takes his shot."

"You've made a lot of people angry, Wade."

"I know." But there was only one person whose opinion mattered: Samantha. If she could find it in her heart to forgive him and trust him again, he'd be able to live with the rest of the world hating his guts.

"I have a bit more to say about Morrissey." Hurtado had returned to his all-important agenda. "The nature of the relationship between an agent and a snitch is a complicated one. At times, I praised him and offered him bribes. The reverse was also true. And I had to keep in mind that a snitch is, by his very nature, a liar who is without loyalty and…"

He droned on with his lecture. The matching set of agents he'd brought with him listened intently. Wade was glad to see that Ty wasn't similarly impressed. He'd left his chair beside the desk and stood at the window, gazing out at the front porch.

As Wade took a position beside him, he wondered if his pal Ty was thinking about what he'd given up on the ranch by following a career in the FBI. From where they stood, they could see the barn, the horses in the corral and Papa Baxter leaning against the fence with his head tilted to catch the warmth of the sun. It was a good life.

If Ty wanted to continue with the feds, he needed to become a supervisory agent real soon. He'd do a better job than Hurtado. Ty was smart and motivated and hadn't yet been consumed by the bureaucracy.

At the far end of the fence, Wade saw one of the Swain County Sheriff's Department vehicles turn onto the driveway. Near the house, the vehicle swerved and parked next to Samantha's SUV. Wade still couldn't tell who it was.

Ty groaned. "It's Caleb."

Any hope of claiming he was dead vanished. The rumor that he was still alive had spread faster than the wildfire. When he saw Deputy Caleb Schmidt jump out of his car and charge toward the front door, Wade pivoted and spoke to Hurtado. "If there's anything important I should know, tell me now."

Hurtado gave an annoyed huff. "Obviously, you're incapable of being patient. At least try to be courteous."

"Sir," Ty said as he stepped forward. "We're about

to be interrupted by Caleb Schmidt, a man who doesn't know the meaning of silence."

"One more thing from Morrissey," Hurtado said. "Before he was killed, the snitch told me there was something big going down."

Again, old news. Ty had already mentioned the smuggling of stolen weapons from the US Army base. "Did he have any details?"

"No location, but a time. Tomorrow night between nine and midnight."

The office door crashed open. Caleb came strutting inside with his thumbs hitched in his belt loops. In spite of his attempt to act cool, his breathing was rapid. His thick glasses were slightly askew. When he saw Wade, he froze.

Wade ground his rear molars together, preparing himself to be read the Caleb Schmidt version of the riot act. Instead, the old man flung his scrawny arms around Wade for a quick but ferocious hug.

"Glad to see you," Caleb muttered.

"Glad to be seen."

"If you ever pull a stunt like that again, I will kill you. I mean it. I don't make none of them there idle threats."

In his position, Wade would have felt the same.

Chapter Eighteen

After a heart-to-heart talk with Maggie Baxter, Sam found a quiet corner in an upstairs bedroom—the blue one with clouds painted across the ceiling—to call her parents. She had decided not to lie but to tell them as little as possible. Somehow, that plan got her started on an endless loop.

"Here's the deal, Dad. I need you and Mom to keep Jenny safe for a few days, a week at most."

"I thought you had a problem with the fire."

"The fire is ninety percent contained."

"Then it's okay if we bring Jenny back home."

That conclusion brought her back to "keep Jenny safe for a few days." And the circle started anew.

Her dad asked, "What kind of trouble are you in?"

She tried to demur. "I'd rather not say."

"I don't like that, Sammy girl, don't like it at all. I'm going to hire us a rental car, and we're heading back there as quick as we can."

"Stop!" There didn't seem to be an easy, gentle way to handle explosive news. "I don't want to lie to you."

"You'd better not."

"You've got to promise me, from the depths of your

heart, that you won't tell Jenny. She needs to hear this from me. In person."

"I promise."

She tried one more time to get him to change his mind, but he steadfastly refused. She decided to pull the pin on this grenade and let fly. "Wade isn't dead."

"Huh?"

"He faked his death and has been in witness protection."

"Huh?"

"There are some very dangerous cartel people after him, and he pretended to be dead so Jenny and I would be safe."

After a long pause, her dad said, "Run this by me again."

She told him again, filling in more of the blanks, and then again and again until finally he started repeating parts back to her, including the all-important promise not to tell Jenny.

"I won't bring Jenny back home," he said, "but I'm going to hire a rental car and stay within easy driving distance of your house until my Cessna is fixed. If you need this old cop, call me. I'll be there in just a few hours."

She figured that was the best assurance she could get. "You aren't old and you're a great lawman. Dad, you're the only cop I'd trust with my little girl."

After she disconnected the call, she pulled aside the blue curtain and looked out the window to the driveway in front of the ranch house. Two Swain County Sheriff's Department vehicles, including the gas-saving hybrid they were testing, drove toward the house. Then she noticed Deputy Schmidt's SUV parked next to hers. She had only six deputies. At least four of them were here.

The ace lawmen of Swain County had somehow figured out that Wade was alive and well and hanging out at the Baxter ranch. Would she be expected to coordinate with them? More likely, the boys would circle around Wade and beg him to come back and save them from the mean lady sheriff who made them take target practice once a week and insisted that paperwork be filed before they went home for the night.

She really didn't want to argue. If they wanted her gone, she'd go. Taking on the responsibilities of the sheriff's job had seemed like a good thing at the time. But it was thankless work, and she was tired. She pulled down the shades on the windows, closed the curtains and turned out the lights.

This bedroom had been designed for a child with the soothing blue color and the fluffy clouds painted overhead, but it was exactly what Sam needed—a comforting place where all the conflict and noises were locked out. She stretched out on one of the two twin-size beds. With the room darkened, the clouds on the ceiling became luminous decals of stars, a simple but magical detail.

The door handle turned, and her very own Prince Charming entered the room. While she was lying down and looking up, Wade seemed so tall that the top of his head brushed the stars. So handsome, he was strong enough to slay any dragon.

He sat on the edge of the twin bed and stroked a tendril of hair off her forehead. "You washed your hair."

"I smelled like a stinky old fireplace."

"And you changed clothes." He caught hold of the zipper pull on the orange Broncos sweatshirt she'd snatched from Ty's dresser. Wade tugged the zip lower. "Maybe you should try a different outfit."

"Are you being suggestive?"

"Should I be more obvious?" He gave a decisive yank on the zipper.

She slapped his hand, sat up on the bed and pulled the zipper back up. "This is a safe, magical room, made for a child. An innocent room. Do you see the stars on the ceiling? They're watching us."

"And so is everybody else. All the Swain County deputies, led by Caleb, are here."

"I saw part of the convoy arriving. I bet they're excited to see you."

"And ticked off." He exhaled a sigh. "That seems to be the typical response. I'm the guy everybody hates to love."

"An apt description," she said. He wasn't even trying to be agreeable, but she was nodding her head. "How was your talk with Hurtado?"

"I don't like the supervisory special agent any more than you do."

"You know what *SSA* spells backward?" She chuckled at her little joke. "You probably know him a lot better than I do. Every time I've talked to him, he's been phony."

"He's smug and arrogant. He acts like he's the big expert, but he's done a really poor job in getting this smuggling operation shut down. Morrissey was his snitch."

"And what did Morrissey tell him?"

"Here's the only useful piece of information. The

weapons that were stolen from the army base are going to be exchanged tomorrow night between nine and midnight."

"And we don't know where," she said. Otherwise, the FBI could call in the troops and set a trap.

"Not a clue."

He pushed himself off the bed and started pacing. In the dimly lit room, he looked like a muscular but confused shadow trying to decide where to alight.

She turned on the bedside lamp and got another lovely surprise. The lampshade rotated and flashed light silhouettes on the walls while a music box played "Hush, Little Baby."

"Adorable," she said. "I want Maggie to come to our house and decorate a room like this."

"For Jenny?"

"Maybe not. Our little Jenny wants to be a big girl who gets to do big-girl things. Like I told you, she wants to learn how to snowboard and ride horses. Doesn't have much use for playing with babyish things."

"Does she still like Gordo?"

"Of course." Her daddy had given her that special stuffed animal—a plump hippo with a goofy grin. "She can't go to sleep without Gordo."

"I can't wait to sit down with her and listen to one of her long, rambling stories. And I want to read to her, even if she wants the same book again and again. And yes to the horses. I'll teach my girl to snowboard and to ski."

When they talked about simple family things, it was as though he'd never left. They could pick up where they'd left off and move forward…except for the deadly threat on all their lives.

She couldn't lie back and enjoy the fake stars over-head. They needed answers. She gave herself a kick in the butt. "Did Hurtado have any plans?"

"I don't know. I left the briefing when he was only halfway through his agenda. But I have an idea. When Caleb showed up, I got inspired."

"I'm shocked, totally shocked." She rolled her eyes. "That has to be the first time in recorded history that the words *Caleb* and *inspired* were used in the same sentence."

"Unlikely? Yes. But this might be a bit of genius."

"Tell."

He sat on the other twin bed, placed his elbows on his knees and leaned toward her. "Do you think any of our deputies are part of the smuggling operation?"

The possibility had never presented itself in her mind. She had to think about it. There were different charac-teristics to different law-enforcement groups. The state patrol was standoffish and tended to be Lone Rangers. Undercover guys, like the men who worked for the DEA and ATF, were very cool and faced temptations every day. Aspen cops had a status thing going, while the Grand Junction law enforcement considered themselves to be more urban.

The small bunch that worked for the Swain County Sheriff's Department weren't cool or shiny or tough. They were earnest, tried to do the right thing and were a little bit nerdy.

She shrugged. "Nobody approached me to join their smuggling operations. Were you ever invited to that party?"

He shook his head. "I'd like to think it was my ster-ling rep as a straight shooter that kept the criminals from recruiting me, but I think it was more a matter of being in the wrong place at the right time."

"And your friendship with Ty," she reminded him. "If somebody approached you and you turned them down, Ty and the FBI would know about it."

"Whatever the reason," he said, "I think we can trust our deputies and the dispatchers."

"You could be right about that. What does that prove?"

"If anybody can sniff out crime in Swain County, it's our guys. We know *when* the next exchange of goods is taking place. All we need to do is find out *where*."

Talk about a long shot! Six deputies plus the two of them would try to find the roots of a smuggling operation in the hundred-and-sixty-square-mile area of Swain County, plus the neighboring counties that included hundreds of miles more of open territory. If by some crazy chance they actually found the smugglers, what would this hapless band do to take them down?

She got off the bed, took his hands and pulled him to his feet. "I guess we've got to start somewhere."

"And I have a plan B."

"Of course you do."

"The success of it depends on you," he said. "How's your relationship with Lieutenant Natchez?"

"Earlier today, I fired two bullets at him."

"Perfect."

WADE GATHERED HIS ragtag army of six deputies around the long table in the bunkhouse behind the ranch. The big two-story house where Maggie Baxter ran things was tidy, efficient and nicely decorated. The bunkhouse, which was full only a couple of times a year when they hired on extra help, was a barracks-like man cave with very little attempt at decoration and two wide-screen televisions, one at either end of the long structure.

The refrigerator was well stocked with beer. And Maggie had been kind enough to provide this law-enforcement crew with sandwiches, chips and two fresh-baked apple pies. Mama Baxter was on their side; Wade wished he could say the same for Ty and the FBI. Hurtado had warned him that they were dealing with a vicious cartel. Blood might be spilled. They had virtually no chance of success.

At least Wade and his band of misfits were taking action.

Their first order of business was food. Three or four ranch hands were also at the table, and everybody helped themselves.

Wade was surprised when Logan came through the door with two other guys. Ty's brother slapped Wade on the back and made introductions.

"What's this about?" Wade asked.

"Some of these men might want to help."

He lowered his voice. "I can't ask them to put their lives in danger."

"Did you forget that this is the West? The place where the locals form a posse and ride out after the bank robbers? Maybe we're not as wild as in the olden days, but we take care of our neighbors."

"What are you saying?"

"You might have a lot more deputies than you realize."

An unexpected turn of events, but he welcomed the extra help. Sitting at the table, he looked over at the two youngest deputies, both in their twenties. These two small-town boys were skillful when it came to search-and-rescue operations. Local motorists loved these guys.

Caleb Schmidt took a seat at Wade's left. As the man with the most seniority, he had standing. And he never lacked for enthusiasm or an opinion.

Samantha was talking quietly to the three other deputies, the men who thought of police work as their career, not because they harbored a passion for justice but rather they saw this as a steady job with decent benefits and an opportunity to help. He'd noticed that these three looked to Samantha for decision-making. Her rational style of leadership appealed to them.

After they dug into the food and beer, Wade stood at the end of the table. He wanted them to know what they were getting into. And he wanted to give them a chance to back out.

"One more time," he said, "I apologize to each and every one of you for inconveniences my death might have caused. My intention was never to hurt. I thought I was protecting my family and my friends."

"We heard you," Caleb said. "No more apologies."

"Before we get started," he said, "I want you all to know that this could be dangerous. One of our enemies in this smuggling operation is the Esteban cartel. This criminal organization has multinational reach. The scope of their cruelty and violence cannot be fully described. They've slaughtered whole villages of men, women and children. They're responsible for beheadings and mutilations. These are the monsters that haunt our nightmares, incapable of redemption or reason."

He looked up and down the table. Every person was quiet, thoughtful.

"The other end of this smuggling operation is even

more terrifying. You wouldn't know they were monsters. They look like us. Most of them are lawmen—cops, federal agents, state employees. You've been to parties with them, maybe even had them over to your house."

He thought of that barbecue at his home where Morrissey and Natchez were guests. "Most of you know that a state patrolman named Drew Morrissey was murdered. A big, friendly guy, he was a goof-off. And he was part of this smuggling operation. Not because he was particularly evil or cruel. He did it for one reason."

"For the money," Caleb said. "We've all been tempted. Makes me want to puke when I stop a speeder and he passes me a twenty with his driver's license and registration. That's how it starts. You take one little bribe and before you know it, you're working for the cartel."

Wade couldn't have said it better himself. He shook Caleb's hand. "I want to rip this smuggling operation apart. They've been working in Swain County and nearby areas for quite a while. I want them gone."

The two young deputies stood. "We're with you, Wade."

"The Baxters have been real understanding about letting us meet here. They've got the FBI in the parlor and us in the bunkhouse." Which, he thought, was appropriate. "If you want to be part of what I'm putting together, come to my house by three o'clock."

Samantha stood. "There's no shame in deciding you don't want to take on the monsters of the world. It's the sane decision. Nobody will think less of you if you don't show."

Wade stepped forward, took her hand and left the bunkhouse.

Chapter Nineteen

Sam hauled an armful of supplies into the kitchen of their house. Wade came behind her with more groceries. In their past life together, they entertained often, so she knew how to grab enough munchies to feed an army.

But this wasn't going to be a party. They wouldn't be playing games or trying to match up their single friends. She would probably be the only woman here, and none of the men thought of her that way, except Wade. She permitted herself a little smile. That was as it should be.

Their house would be the base of operations for tracking down the smugglers. That was, of course, if anyone showed up. Wade had given an inspiring speech, but he'd also been honest about the risks.

"Do you think anybody is going to show?" she asked.

"Caleb, for sure."

"I thought we should put him in charge of communications. Somebody needs to stay here and coordinate information."

He unloaded a few boxes of snack food into the large pantry between the kitchen and the mudroom. "I was hoping that you'd take on that responsibility."

Irritated, she placed a two-pound package of deli-sliced peppered turkey in the fridge and frowned at him.

"Do you want me to stay here because you don't think I can handle fieldwork? Or is it so I won't get hurt?"

"You want the truth?" he asked.

"Always." That was the only way she could trust him.

"I want to protect you. That doesn't mean I don't think you're capable. It's an instinct."

"Well, get over it." She placed bananas and Granny Smith apples in a bowl. "You're going to have to learn how to let me take care of myself. The same goes for Jenny. She's growing up and needs to be independent."

He threw up his hands. "Are you telling me I'm not allowed to take care of our little girl?"

"Taking care of her is one thing, but don't be a helicopter dad, always hovering around her."

"As it so happens," he said, "I know the meaning of that term. People in witness protection tend to watch a lot of television. And don't worry—I won't hover."

She shot him a grin. "I guess you're up on all the parenting techniques."

"Speaking of parents," he said, "you've had a couple of conversations with yours. What's up?"

She explained about the mechanical problems with the Cessna and then moved on to a deeper issue. "I told Dad that you're still alive."

He winced. "How angry is he?"

"That wasn't his response. He wants to help catch the bad guys. Just like all these other people from the Baxter ranch."

"We know good people," he said.

Caleb was the first to arrive, and he immediately made himself useful by brewing a pot of coffee.

Sam dashed upstairs to change clothes and put her hair in a braid so it wouldn't get in the way. After she'd thrown on a fresh pair of jeans and a white tank top under a plaid shirt, she checked her reflection in the mirror. She looked tough and competent, which was how she wanted Wade to see her.

Their extra-long bed stretched out in front of her like a promise. She couldn't wait until they were lying together in each other's arms, couldn't wait to hear him whisper her name, *Samantha, Samantha*. By the time she came downstairs again, three other deputies had arrived, and her house had been turned into a strategic battlefield. A huge topographical map was laid out on the dining room table. Quadrants marked off areas that should be searched.

The obvious problem was that they needed more people. The square miles to be covered were vast. And they were only a measly few.

Trying to narrow and focus their search, every man put in his bits of information. They actually knew a great deal. Being a deputy meant spending time in uncharted territory where people got lost or had cars break down. Where were the abandoned houses like the ones at Hanging Rock? Were there rental sites available? How was the fire going to impact their search?

"We don't know what the smugglers are going to take in exchange for the illegal arms," Wade said. "Their package could be small, like prescription drugs. Or it could be a truckload of human beings."

"What size are the weapons?" one of the deputies asked.

As they began calculating, she pushed open the sliding glass door and went onto the deck. The smoke from the wildfire was almost gone. A fresh breeze stroked her cheeks.

Then she saw the cars and trucks driving up the road to her house, kicking up a cloud of reddish dust. Logan was in the first truck. He leaned out and waved to her. There were probably five guys in the back of his truck. Four more cars brought up the rear. Wade's speech had been effective.

In the dining room, an air of solidarity prevailed. Plotting the areas to be searched was greatly enhanced by adding the cowboys from Baxter ranch who could patrol far and wide on horseback. More than once, she heard Wade telling them not to shoot first and ask questions later.

She heard what sounded like the *thwap-thwap-thwap* of a helicopter's rotors and went to the front window. When she saw the FBI chopper dipping down to land on a flat spot near the road, she couldn't believe it.

Wade came up beside her. "What do you think this is about?"

"Let's go find out."

When they walked out the front door, Logan joined them. He nudged Wade's shoulder. "What did I tell you? My brother can't stand being left out."

"I never thought he'd convince his boss."

Ty shoved open the chopper door and came toward them. He stopped a few paces in front of them. "You know that Hurtado does not approve of what I'm doing. Consider the chopper a gift horse, and you should never look a gift horse in the mouth."

"What should we do with it?" Wade asked.

"There's a couple of hours of daylight left," Ty said, "and this is probably the best way to get an overview of the burned acreage. Marshal Hobbs isn't going to let you go exploring on foot."

"I'll go with you," Logan said, stepping forward. "I've been thinking about getting one of these for the ranch. This could be a test drive. I'll be back here after dusk."

She watched them walk downhill toward the whirring blades. "Family is everything."

He nodded. "I need to call my sister."

"She is so totally going to kick your butt. Maybe you could record the call for me."

"Much as I hate to interrupt the fun time you're having by treating me like a jerk, I have another project for you."

"Natchez." She'd been thinking about him since Wade brought his name up. "Why me? And what do you want from him?"

"In case you hadn't noticed," he said, "he's real uncomfortable around you. Because the man is a fool, I think he underestimates you."

"Do you think he's one of the smugglers?"

"I'm willing to bet that good old Natchez has had a taste for the payoffs."

"What should I do?"

"Call him, and tell him that you hate my guts and you want to get out of this one-horse town. Tell him you want to make some serious cash, to meet with the smugglers."

"Will he believe that?"

"If you sell it right, he'll believe anything."

She appreciated that he was sending her off on a solo mission. "With all your protective instincts, I'm kind of surprised that you're willing to let me handle this on my own."

"Who said you'd be alone?"

Wade's bright idea was for him to hide in the car with her. After she got Natchez to talk, Wade would help her arrest him. Though she wouldn't admit it to him, she was relieved that he'd be close. Natchez acted the fool. But his swearing and intense tidiness might be a cover. He was organized enough to be the ringleader.

She placed the call. To her surprise, Natchez answered.

"I expected to get voice mail," she said.

"I always answer my calls," he said. "It's efficient. I expect you're calling about Morrissey's murder, and I've got nothing to report."

This wasn't going well. She needed to develop a more personal relationship. What was his first name? "You know, Trevor, I don't really mind when you swear."

"I'll be damned. Are you a dirty girl?"

"Maybe." She'd need a long soak in a scented bath after this conversation. "My husband doesn't understand that. I wish he'd had the good sense to stay dead."

After repeated swearing, he said, "You're kind of a surprise."

"There's something you might be able to help me with, Trevor," she purred into the phone. "I'm tired of living in this boring little burg. I want to make some cash, some real cash."

"I think I know what you're talking about," he said. "And there's no way I'd introduce you to those people."

Gotcha! "So you know who they are?"

"I didn't say that."

"But you did, Trevor. You said 'those people.'" And he sounded as if they were beneath him. Was he talking about the cartel or the locals? "I knew you'd be able to help me. You're well connected."

"I should go," he said.

She could almost hear him backpedaling over the phone. She had to offer him something special to keep him interested. "You know, with all these FBI guys running around, a girl tends to overhear things."

"What FBI guys?"

"You can see them flying around in their black helicopter. Take a gander out your window."

"I see them."

"If you introduce me to the people who can make me big bucks, I promise the FBI won't get in the way of the big deal that's going down tomorrow night."

"You know about tomorrow night?"

"Like I said, I hear things." She'd done the selling. Now she needed to be a closer. "Meet me tonight, Trevor. I'll come to your place."

"I don't know." Nerves trembled in his voice. "I just don't know."

"This is a onetime offer. I want an introduction that gets me into the smuggling operation."

"Okay, okay. You're on."

They arranged to meet tonight at ten o'clock at the Pine Cone Motel on the far end of Woodridge. When she ended the call, she couldn't help wondering. Were men really that gullible? Or did she have a creepy undercover talent that she'd never used before?

For the rest of the day and into the night, she helped Caleb send their guys out into the field and recorded when they reported back. The ranch hands were having the most fun playing posse. They each took a horse and went about fifteen miles from the Baxter ranch. There wasn't much farther they could go and make it back before nightfall.

The only viable leads came from what they observed when looking down from higher elevations. They pinpointed two ranches with high activity. When the deputies drove to the ranches to check them out, they found that one was having a family reunion and the other had set up a kitchen to feed the firefighters.

By nine o'clock, she was exhausted. Flirting with Trevor Natchez sounded like less fun than scrubbing toilets. First, she put in a good-night call to Jenny. Then she checked in with the fire marshal, who said the fire was still 90 percent contained, which meant he and his crew would be sticking around for a while longer.

At half past, she was in her SUV, with Wade lying across the seats in the back. He had tried to scrunch down on the passenger side, but his extra-large body wasn't meant to be concealed so easily.

"When we get there," he said, "you don't have to play any games with him. I don't like that he wanted you to come to a motel. What did you say to the guy, anyway?"

"I might have hinted that I thought his endless dirty talk was kind of sexy."

Wade groaned. "Leave your phone turned on so I can hear what's happening. You want to get the location for the smugglers' drop. And the name of the ringleader."

Not exactly an easy assignment. "And if he doesn't want to talk to me?"

"Back to the drawing board."

The Pine Cone Motel was full, as she expected it would be. The firefighters needed to have someplace to sleep. Natchez hadn't given her a room number, but his spotless Crown Vic was parked outside number seven, and a light shone from inside.

After syncing her phone with Wade's, she got out of

her car, went to Natchez's room and tapped on the door. "Trevor? Open up. It's me."

He didn't answer her knock, but the door moved inward when she pushed. It hadn't been properly closed. She snatched her hand away as though she'd touched a hot stove. Why would he leave the door open? Was he getting ice from the machine down the hall?

"I don't like this," she said aloud so Wade could hear. "Don't like it at all."

He was out of the SUV in a flash. His weapon was drawn and he tapped her holster to remind her that this might be a good time to be armed. Her fingers trembled as she wrapped them around the grip of her gun.

Wade shoved the door open. He went in hard and hot.

Natchez's body was neatly centered on the beige floral bedspread. There were two holes in his chest, just like Morrissey, but this was the primary crime scene. The state patrolman's uniform and the bed were saturated with blood.

She hadn't expected to scream.

Chapter Twenty

Wade pulled Samantha close and held her while she cut loose with a loud, piercing scream. He didn't blame her; the scene was horrific. Natchez lay in stillness. His eyes were closed. His face was peaceful. It looked as if he'd been sleeping when he was shot. The gore erupted across his chest, so much blood.

Samantha hiccuped a few sobs and stepped back, trying to regain control. "W-w-we should check his phone."

On the table beside the bed, they found his keys and his cell phone. The history of use showed that his only calls were between himself and his dispatcher and, of course, the call from Samantha. Natchez must have used a burner phone to communicate with the ringleader. Wade was certain that was who'd killed him. The ringleader was calling the shots.

A familiar face peered around the edge of the doorjamb. "Hello. Is anything wrong?"

Justin Hobbs stepped over the threshold, glanced at the body on the bed and averted his gaze. "My God."

"Are you staying here?" Wade asked.

"With many of the other firefighters." Hobbs peered at him, then blinked twice. His beard seemed to stand on end as he stared. "You're Wade, Sam's husband. I thought you were dead."

"I should explain," Samantha said.

As she walked toward him, her legs nearly buckled. She'd been through enough for one day. Dealing with this murder, which was clearly in Swain County jurisdiction, was going to take some time and coordinated effort. Natchez was a jerk, but his death needed to be investigated the right way.

Wade followed her and Hobbs outside. "I can handle this," he said. "Why don't you go home. Maybe Marshal Hobbs would be nice enough to give you a ride."

"I need to stay. I'm the sheriff, after all." Fighting back tears, she said, "Another murder investigation. That's got to be a record."

"It's not your fault," Wade said.

"This one is. He was in the wrong place at the wrong time, and I put him there." She leaned against the side of her SUV and glanced between the two men. "I'm in over my head. I'm drowning."

He'd never seen her so overwhelmed. Gently, he guided her to the SUV and opened the door to the bench seat in the rear. "I want you to lie down, Samantha. Get some sleep. You need it."

When he returned to the motel room where Natchez had been murdered, the fire marshal followed. Hobbs asked, "Anything I can do to help?"

"Thanks, but this is my problem."

"If you don't mind my asking, why did you pretend to be dead?"

"Witness protection." Wade knew he was being terse, but he'd told this story too many times already.

"Now the trial must be over, right?"

"Not exactly, but they have other evidence. My testimony isn't as important." Before the barrel-chested firefighter who actually resembled Smokey the Bear shuffled back to his room, Wade called out, "Do you have the fire contained?"

"It's just a couple of hot spots."

Wade reached into his pocket and pulled out his phone. Following Samantha's example at the Morrissey scene, he took photos of the crime scene. There didn't appear to be a murder weapon. He contacted the ambulance from Glenwood Springs and called Ty to ask about using the FBI crime lab for the autopsy.

He went through the procedures as though a murder investigation was something he did every day, talking to the manager in the motel office who hadn't seen anything strange and didn't have surveillance cameras. He interviewed several people who were staying at the Pine Cone Motel. Several came out of their rooms to see what had happened. Nobody saw anything useful.

When all of this was over, quiet little Swain County was going to have an exceptionally experienced forensic crew. On the other hand, he hoped these were skills he'd never have to use again.

Every so often, he'd check on Samantha sleeping in the back of her SUV with a blanket pulled up over her head. She needed the rest, desperately needed it. When he finally had all the details taken care of and the ambulance was carrying the body to Denver for autopsy, Wade climbed behind the wheel of her SUV.

He didn't want to drive with her lying on the seat; she'd fall off if he came to a sudden stop. "Come on, sleepy girl, wake up."

She didn't move, not an inch. What was wrong? Was

she sick? If anything had happened to her, he couldn't face it, couldn't go on. His sorry life would be over.

Leaping from the front seat, he went to the back and threw open the door. He grabbed a handful of blanket. Nothing there. She was gone.

A scrap of notebook paper fluttered to the ground. The writing was so sloppy that he could hardly read it.

If you want to see her alive, back off. No more search. No more trouble.

If this note came from the cartel, Samantha was already as good as dead. An empty feeling in the pit of his belly grew until numbness consumed his entire body. He was a shell, without strength or breath. He had lost the will to live.

He sank down on the curb outside the room where Natchez had been murdered. In a terrible irony, he knew for the first time what she'd gone through when he faked his death. And he couldn't tell her. This was the worst moment of his life, the greatest pain.

How could he lose her?

SAM COULDN'T SEE a thing. Her head was covered with a black hood, and duct tape covered her mouth. She inhaled through her nostrils, slowly, and then she exhaled. Accomplishing this simple act gave her great satisfaction, and she did it again.

Not yet awake, she felt as if she was caught at the edge of a nightmare and couldn't wake up. This couldn't be reality. It made no sense for her to be riding in the back of a truck with blankets piled on top of her. Where was she going?

She'd been drugged. That would explain why her brain was foggy. The last thing she remembered was falling asleep in the back of her car. No, wait—she remembered blood. There was a murder, another murder. The front of his uniform was drenched in blood. How could that be? If he was shot in the chest and didn't move, the blood would drain through the exit wounds in his back. He must have struggled, thrashed around. And then the killer arranged his body.

That scenario seemed worse. The kind of killer who could stand back and watch a man die was more sadistic than someone who came in, fired and left. Both were murderers. Both were horrible.

And she had to face the dawning realization that the murderer had bound her wrists and ankles. She was in the back of his truck. She could only hope that he would end her life quickly with two neat bullets to the chest.

Chapter Twenty-One

When he returned to the house, Wade spoke to no one. His private grief weighed too heavily on his shoulders. He could hardly make it upstairs to his bedroom, where he fell onto their extra-long bed. This was his fault. There was no one else he could blame.

He had taken his eyes off Samantha. Now she was gone.

His phone rang, and he snatched it, hoping to see that she was calling, imagining that she would tell him she was all right. It was an Unknown Caller.

He answered. "Who is this?"

"It's Ty. Where are you?"

"Why do you want to know?"

From the start, Wade had known that he should suspect Ty. Even if he was an old friend and they'd grown up together, it didn't mean that Ty hadn't taken on another role. He could be the ringleader.

There were three strikes against him. First, Ty was the one who came up with the faked-death scene. Second, he was high on the food chain in law enforcement. Third, he knew many of the locals from growing up in Swain County.

Having Ty turn out to be the ringleader might be a

positive thing because he loved Samantha and would never hurt her. Wade modulated his voice, removing all trace of hostility. "I'm home. I came directly here from the motel. Are you checking up on me? Making sure I'm not searching?"

"Something's wrong with you," Ty said. "I'll be there in a couple of minutes."

"Where are you?"

"At the ranch. Where else would I be?"

Being at the ranch didn't prove his innocence. The ringleader could send one of the guys who worked for him to kidnap Samantha. It wouldn't have taken much to grab her. They'd give her a quick poke with a sedative, pick her up and carry her to a waiting vehicle. The operation would take only a couple of minutes.

There had to be something Wade could do, but his brain wasn't working. He lay flat on the bed, staring up at the ceiling, running through suspects. His favorite was Hurtado, mostly because he didn't like the guy.

Everett Hurtado would make an effective ringleader. Not only was he able to misdirect the attentions of the FBI and other federal agencies, but he was accustomed to leadership. His only needs for keeping his dirty business operational were a couple of cell phones. And Hurtado would love the big bucks to be made in smuggling.

Wade ran through a couple of other lawmen. And then he thought of Justin Hobbs. The fire marshal had been on scene at the Pine Cone Motel. He was in frequent communication with Samantha.

Wade recalled the night Hobbs had popped over for a visit. At the time, it seemed as if he was getting ready to hit on Samantha. Maybe he'd been fishing for answers about her husband, trying to find out if Wade was still alive. Tonight when they met, Hobbs seemed surprised that Wade wasn't dead. Was he acting? With that damn beard in the way, who could tell?

Knowledge of his death was of key importance. The ringleader was responsible for the death of Morrissey the snitch and had planned to frame Wade by leaving his Colt .45 revolver at the scene. If that frame was going to work, Wade had to be alive. If Hobbs didn't know, he wasn't the ringleader.

Ty rapped on the bedroom door. "Wade? Are you okay, man? What's going on?"

The final proof appeared in Wade's mind. He had the answer. He hoped he'd be in time to save Samantha.

SAM DIDN'T KNOW how many hours she'd been held captive, but it seemed like a long time. The black hood still covered her head but the room seemed lighter. Dawn was beginning to break through the darkness.

She was lying on a bed. The ropes around her wrists were tethered to the bed frame. Her ankles were tied together but were not fastened to anything else. All of her wriggling around hadn't amounted to much. The cord around her wrists was looser but not enough to get free.

Her only real accomplishment was biting through the duct tape on her mouth so she could breathe. More oxygen to the brain served to sharpen her awareness of how much trouble she'd fallen into.

No doubt, she was a hostage. They were using her for leverage to force Wade's hand.

She scooted around on the bed so she was sitting near the frame, which seemed like a less vulnerable position than lying flat. If she could get the black hood off her face, she'd be able to gnaw at the cords.

The hood lifted as high as her chin. Twisting awkwardly and flipping her head, she got it higher. Finally, it was off. The dim light of early morning flooded her eyes.

She was in a small bedroom, lying on dirty sheets in a double bed. There were no photographs or pictures on the dull beige walls. Looking through the one window, she could tell that she was on the first floor. Though she couldn't see any other houses from the window, she called for help.

After her first hoarse shout, she waited. She hadn't heard anybody walking around in a long time. Had her captor left her here alone? She gave another yell.

Her throat was scratchy. The inside of her mouth tasted like cotton. If he had left her alone, it was certain that there were no nearby neighbors.

She concentrated on the cords that fastened her wrists to the bed frame.

BEFORE HE LEFT the house, Wade told Caleb to lie for him and tell anybody who called that he couldn't be reached. He pressed one of his last burner phones into Caleb's hand. "Then you call and tell me who is trying to find me."

"You can count on me."

Wade looked the aged deputy up and down. He was holding up better than most of the crew. He said, "I trust you." And he meant it.

He jumped into Ty's sleek black SUV. "We're going to Woodridge. To the courthouse."

Ty took off. "Do you mind telling me what we're doing? I know something's wrong. Where's Sam?"

Wade wasn't answering any questions until he had his proof. As far as he was concerned, Ty was still a suspect. "Why did you call me?"

"I wanted to let you know that we had an FBI forensic doctor at the Glenwood hospital. He did a preliminary autopsy on Natchez. The bullets that killed him came from a different gun than those that killed Morrissey."

Old news. "How much do you know about Justin Hobbs?"

"According to Mama, he's a real catch. If you hadn't returned from the dead, old Justin would have been making a play for Sam."

Wade hoped Hobbs's affection for Sam was real. He'd be less likely to hurt her. If he was the ringleader…

Ty parked in front of the courthouse and they dashed up the wide stone steps to the front door. Using Samantha's keys, Wade opened the front door. In the sheriff's office, he found what he was looking for. Among the many photographs of community groups, he located a picture that had been playing in the back of his mind since that day in Austin when he saw a familiar face.

Here he was…the face Wade had seen…the man he didn't know who had changed his life. He stood front and center in a group photo of a volunteer fire brigade. Standing beside him was Justin Hobbs.

"He's the ringleader," Wade said, "and he's holding Samantha hostage."

SAM HEARD THE noise from another part of the house. A door slammed. She heard him approaching her bedroom. It was too late to put the hood back on, but she didn't want to see the person who walked through the door. Her chance of survival would be significantly better if she didn't know him.

The bedroom door creaked open. "Good morning, Sam. I have a surprise for you."

"Justin?" She opened her eyes and looked into his heavily bearded face. "Could you untie me? My feet are numb."

"Wait until I tell you my news. After that, I'm guessing that you won't want to escape."

The hell I won't! Sam didn't care about the smuggling or the cartel or any of these other things. She just wanted to survive, wanted her life with Wade back.

Hobbs held up her telephone and pressed the play button. Jenny's voice came through loud and clear.

"Hi, Mommy," she said. "We're coming to see you right away. The fire marshal who came to my school last year and talked about fire safety gave us directions."

Sam's heart ached. "How could you?"

"It's about time that one of those school programs paid off."

"You tricked my daughter into trusting you."

"And your father, too." Hobbs checked his wristwatch. "They ought to be here in half an hour. Your father is quite the guy. He's been hovering around this area since yesterday, waiting to rush in and save the day. Reminds me of Wade. That's the kind of guy you like, right?"

"Tell me what you want." She would do anything to protect her daughter. "Just leave Jenny out of it."

"I want the money from this last smuggling score. All you have to do is stay here with your mom and dad and little Jenny, and don't tell anybody where the exchange will take place."

"Yes." She nodded vigorously. "I'll do whatever you say."

"That's the right attitude," he said. "I've got a little retirement home in Mexico where I'll be very comfortable."

She suppressed the hatred rising inside her as she looked down at the cords that bound her wrists. "Untie me, please."

"I don't have to tell you that if you try anything, it won't go well for Jenny."

"I understand."

"Even if you disable me, there are plenty of people who work for me. Four or five of them are coming here very soon. You'll like them. They're dressed as firefighters."

"Is that how you moved your men from place to place?"

"Everybody loves a firefighter." He started working on the knots that tied her ankles. "I'd give them a uniform and tell them not to talk much."

"May I ask a question?" She twisted her neck to see him. "Who broke into my house and stole Wade's gun?"

"That was Morrissey. I heard from an informant that your husband was the big-deal secret witness. I knew we had to do something when he escaped custody. I figured his first move would be to come home."

Her ankles were free. She struggled to wiggle her toes. It was going to take a little while to get the circulation back. "Who was your informant?"

"Doesn't matter," he said as he pulled the hood completely off her head and stripped off the remnants of the duct tape. "Morrissey stole the gun from your house, Wade's fancy copper-inlaid revolver. It was the perfect thing to use in framing your husband. All I needed was a dead body. Standing right there in front of me was a snitch for the FBI."

"Morrissey."

"I shot him in the back of my truck and drove him to the scene, setting up the supposed accident. I left some guys there to stage an ambush. The plan was for you or Ty to survive, and you'd have to arrest Wade based on the evidence."

"The gun," she said, remembering her mental struggle about hiding it. "How did you know I'd be in that area?"

"You told me all about it when we were calling back and forth. You told me where you were, and I set you up, Sam, told you about the hikers and directed you into the trap. I'm kind of surprised you didn't figure it out."

"I should have."

Before he started untying her hands, he took his handgun from the waistband of his jeans and placed it on the bedside. It was a powerful temptation. She thought about playing the innocent, trying to win his sympathy until she could grab the gun. Then what? He'd still have Jenny.

Her hands were free. He stepped back, leaving his gun unprotected. Too obvious. "Is this a test?"

"And you pass," he said as he snatched his gun. "Let's play house, Sam. I've got some eggs and bacon in the kitchen. Make me breakfast."

Visions of hot grease flying across the room danced behind her eyelids as she stumbled on her clumsy, frozen legs into a small outer room.

Behind her back, she heard him snap a clip into his automatic gun. "It wasn't loaded," she said.

"I'm not a fool."

The gun was now loaded and lethal. If she had another chance to get her hands on it, she could even the playing field. In the kitchen, there were many implements, like knives and heavy frying pans, that she could use to disable him.

Hurting him wasn't enough. If he had the slightest chance to take control again, he would harm her daughter. The only way she could be sure Jenny was safe would be to kill Hobbs.

His men would be here soon. She needed to act before they got here. Instead of attacking him, she took the carton of eggs from the refrigerator. "How many will be eating?"

"Make it scrambled eggs for five." He chuckled. "Aren't you going to ask me about the fire at Hanging Rock?"

He'd mentioned the cabins, but it was Wade's idea to go there and look around. "I suppose you had the cabin all set to start the fire."

"I'm a pro," he said.

From outside the house, she heard gunfire. Jenny! "What's that? What are they shooting at?"

As he went to the front window, he kept his gun aimed at her. "My men are shooting at something."

She silently prayed. *Not my parents. Not Jenny.*

"I know that fancy-ass black SUV," he said. "It's your friend Ty. And look who he's got with him."

She didn't hesitate, not for one more second. With the outstanding aim of a woman who'd played softball every year of her life since she was six, she fired an egg at his face, then another and another. When he reflexively threw up his hands, she whacked him with the frying pan.

Hobbs was a big man. He didn't go down. Blindly, he charged toward her.

Sam was a big woman. She clubbed him again.

He sank onto a knee.

One more time.

He fell flat on his belly.

She grabbed his handgun and went to the front window. When she started firing at Hobbs's men, it was enough of a distraction for Ty and Wade to get them under control. As Ty aimed his semiautomatic rifle at them, the two that were still standing dropped their guns and raised hands over their heads.

Wade rushed toward the porch, and she met him there. He squeezed her tightly in his arms.

"I thought you were dead," he whispered.

"That makes us even."

She kissed him as if there was no tomorrow.

Ty interrupted, "A little help here. I could use some handcuffs."

"I'll get right on it," Wade said. "As soon as I tell this woman that I love her with all my heart."

A small voice called out, "Daddy?"

Sam saw her parents at the edge of the forest. Jenny broke away from them and raced toward her father. He scooped her into his arms and twirled her into the air above his head.

Sam wiped away a tear. Now everything was the way it should be. Their family was complete.

Epilogue

At the end of two full days of paperwork, Sheriff Sam printed the last of her reports and added it to the stack in the center of her desk at the courthouse. Cleaning up after the crime spree in Swain County was a huge job. She had witness statements, doctors' reports and autopsies, ballistics, photographs, arrest records, police reports and much more.

Using both hands, she pushed the stack toward Ty, who sat on the opposite side of her desk. "Here it is. Two murders, Morrissey and Natchez. Both were killed by Justin Hobbs. And I've included ballistics on the antique Colt .45 that Hobbs admitted he used in an attempt to frame Wade for killing Morrissey."

"There was another murder," Ty said, "the guy I shot on the road near the safe house."

"It's in there," she said, "including hospital reports on the other two wounded. Those two and the men Hobbs had at his cabin were all taken into custody and charged with assaulting federal officers. Plus, there were four more smugglers rounded up by the cowboy posse that Wade put together. Not to mention that the posse found the high-tech weaponry that was being smuggled to the Esteban cartel."

"Hobbs had us all fooled."

"All of you. Not me. I knew he was hiding something nasty under his big, thick beard."

"Funny thing," Ty said. "With his beard shaved, he looks like one of the cartel leaders. Blood is thicker than water. Their first contact with him was through family."

"Well, well, imagine that. Bad guys stick together."

Ty chuckled. "Proud of yourself, aren't you?"

"It's not often that a small county sheriff gets to show the FBI how to do their job."

Better yet, she was handing over responsibility for the investigation to the feds. Neither she nor Wade would be targeted by the cartel or the dirty cops. There might be some personal animosity. Sam wouldn't want to be left alone and unguarded in a room with Justin Hobbs, but he was going away for a very long time.

"Your talents—and Wade's—have been duly noted."

"Thank you, Special Agent Baxter." She pointed to the stack. "If the FBI needs copies, there's a machine down the hall outside the mayor's office."

"I'll pick my information off the computer."

"I don't think so." She'd heard horror stories about how hackers were constantly breaking into federal computers. "I don't want you to have access to my equipment."

At that moment, Wade and Jenny entered through the open door to her office. Her husband announced, "Back off, Ty. I'm the only one who gets access to her equipment."

Sam held out her arms and Jenny jumped onto her lap. "What have you and Daddy been up to? I haven't seen you since lunch."

"We went to the Roaring Fork," Jenny said.

That was the river where Wade had supposedly died. She shot him a glance. "I hope you were careful."

"We talked about water safety," Jenny said. "And we saw people in big yellow-and-orange rafts."

They still hadn't told their daughter how it was possible for her father to be dead and then be alive again. Those explanations would have to happen before she went back to school. For right now, Wade was using his time off to reestablish his relationship with his five-year-old daughter. As far as Sam could tell, that connection was going well…better than her own relationship with her husband.

She loved Wade, had never stopped loving him even when he was dead. Her words of forgiveness had been spoken, but it was going to take time for her to let go of her residual pain and anger.

"And we went shopping in Glenwood." Jenny gave her father a mischievous grin and placed her index finger across her lips. "It's a secret."

"Don't tell," he said as he scooped her off her mother's lap and set her down on the floor. "Would you take Ty into the outer office and draw him a picture of the rafters?"

Planting her fists on her skinny hips, she looked up at him. "You just want to talk to Mommy alone."

"Nothing gets past you."

Jenny took Ty's hand and pulled him into the other office. "Shut the door behind you, Uncle Ty. I bet they want to be kissing."

"Do they do that a lot?" Ty teased.

Jenny rolled her eyes. "All the time."

Wade came behind the desk and stood beside her. He gestured toward the paperwork stack. "Is this all of it?"

"Yes!" She blew a long, slow breath through her pursed lips. "In the past week, we've had more crime than in the entire history of Swain County, and that includes a holdup by Butch Cassidy and the Sundance Kid."

"You've been working hard." He flexed his fingers, went behind her chair, pushed her long braid aside and started a neck massage. "How's that feel?"

"Like the touch of an angel." As the tension in her shoulders popped and released, she moaned with pleasure. "A naughty angel."

"Being sheriff is a lot of work."

She'd been meaning to talk to him about the job. When he'd disappeared, he was sheriff. In his absence, she'd been duly elected to the position. "I kind of like it."

"You might want to think twice before you say you'll keep this work." He glided his hands down her arms, leaned down and nibbled at her earlobe, starting a crazy tickle that spread rapidly through her body. "You were almost killed this week."

"Most of the time, I like being sheriff. I'm not ready to retire."

"Glad to hear it," he said.

Though distracted by his touch, she was surprised to hear him agree with her. She rose to her feet, gazed into his light brown eyes and wrapped her arms around his neck. "I thought you wanted to take back your job."

"You're a good sheriff. Everybody says so. And it seems like a shame for you to give that up just because I'm here."

She totally agreed with him. "Why do I get the feeling that you're manipulating me? And if you are, please stop."

He raised his right hand as if taking an oath. "I will

never make plans without consulting you, my wife. Are you ready for a possible plan?"

"Tell me."

"Ty's boss, Everett Hurtado, made me an offer to work with the FBI. I'd get the safe house up and running. They want to use it more for consultations and meetings than as a place for protected witnesses. And they want me to set up an outdoor training program for agents."

"You'd be an FBI agent?"

"A consultant," he said. "Big difference. I wouldn't be involved in active investigations and, therefore, wouldn't be in danger."

This was beginning to sound too good to be true. "What about travel?"

"There might be some, but I'm my own boss and can always refuse to go."

She tasted his lips. "I like this plan of yours."

"I thought you might."

He deepened the kiss, and she experienced the swirling, mind-numbing satisfaction that only Wade could give her. Her body melted against his. Since she wasn't wearing her bulletproof vest today, she could feel the hard muscles of his chest and abdomen.

She exhaled a sigh. "I love you."

"But wait!" He swiveled her chair and sat her down in it. "There's more!"

When he dropped to one knee and took a black velvet box from his pocket, she felt her eyes grow wider and wider until they had to be as big as hubcaps. "What are you doing?"

He showed her the ring. "Samantha Calloway, will you marry me? Again."

"Renew our vows?"

"Yes."

A stunning piece of jewelry, the silver platinum ring glistened and the blue-tinted diamond sparkled. "Did Jenny help you pick this out?"

"She said it had to be blue like your eyes."

Sam slipped the ring on her finger. It was a perfect fit. And so were they.

* * * * *

COMING NEXT MONTH FROM

HARLEQUIN®

INTRIGUE

Available February 16, 2016

#1623 NAVY SEAL SURVIVAL
SEAL of My Own • by Elle James
Navy SEAL Duff Calloway's vacation turns into a dangerous mission when he meets Natalie Layne. She is in Honduras to rescue her sister from human traffickers—not to fall in love with a sexy SEAL.

#1624 STRANGER IN COLD CREEK
The Gates: Most Wanted • by Paula Graves
Agent John Blake is hiding in Cold Creek to recuperate from gunshot wounds. He never expected to thwart an attempt on Miranda Duncan's life—or to find himself falling hard for the no-nonsense deputy.

#1625 GUNNING FOR THE GROOM
Colby Agency: Family Secrets • by Debra Webb & Regan Black
PI Aidan Abbot is undercover as Frankie Leone's fiancé to clear her father's name. But the closer he gets to the truth, the more Aidan wants to protect the woman he was never supposed to fall for.

#1626 SHOTGUN JUSTICE
Texas Rangers: Elite Troop • by Angi Morgan
When a serial killer targets Deputy Avery Travis, it is up to Texas Ranger Jesse Ryder to protect her. But he'll discover that falling for his best friend's little sister is almost as dangerous as the killer stalking them.

#1627 TEXAS HUNT
Mason Ridge • by Barb Han
The man who once traumatized Lisa Moore is back—and he's deadly. Lisa turns to her childhood friend, Ryan Hunt, who risks his life and heart to help. But can Lisa ever truly escape her past?

#1628 PRIVATE BODYGUARD
Orion Security • by Tyler Anne Snell
Bodyguard Oliver Quinn can't deny his history with his new client, PI Darling Smith. But keeping her safe from a killer comes before exploring their lingering feelings.

YOU CAN FIND MORE INFORMATION ON UPCOMING HARLEQUIN® TITLES, FREE EXCERPTS AND MORE AT WWW.HARLEQUIN.COM.

HICNM0216

REQUEST YOUR FREE BOOKS!
2 FREE NOVELS PLUS 2 FREE GIFTS!

HARLEQUIN®

INTRIGUE

BREATHTAKING ROMANTIC SUSPENSE

YES! Please send me 2 FREE Harlequin® Intrigue novels and my 2 FREE gifts (gifts are worth about $10). After receiving them, if I don't wish to receive any more books, I can return the shipping statement marked "cancel." If I don't cancel, I will receive 6 brand-new novels every month and be billed just $4.74 per book in the U.S. or $5.49 per book in Canada. That's a savings of at least 12% off the cover price! It's quite a bargain! Shipping and handling is just 50¢ per book in the U.S. and 75¢ per book in Canada.* I understand that accepting the 2 free books and gifts places me under no obligation to buy anything. I can always return a shipment and cancel at any time. Even if I never buy another book, the two free books and gifts are mine to keep forever.

182/382 HDN GH3D

Name   (PLEASE PRINT)

Address   Apt. #

City   State/Prov.   Zip/Postal Code

Signature (if under 18, a parent or guardian must sign)

Mail to the **Reader Service:**
IN U.S.A.: P.O. Box 1867, Buffalo, NY 14240-1867
IN CANADA: P.O. Box 609, Fort Erie, Ontario L2A 5X3

**Are you a subscriber to Harlequin® Intrigue books
and want to receive the larger-print edition?
Call 1-800-873-8635 or visit www.ReaderService.com.**

* Terms and prices subject to change without notice. Prices do not include applicable taxes. Sales tax applicable in N.Y. Canadian residents will be charged applicable taxes. Offer not valid in Quebec. This offer is limited to one order per household. Not valid for current subscribers to Harlequin Intrigue books. All orders subject to credit approval. Credit or debit balances in a customer's account(s) may be offset by any other outstanding balance owed by or to the customer. Please allow 4 to 6 weeks for delivery. Offer available while quantities last.

Your Privacy—The Reader Service is committed to protecting your privacy. Our Privacy Policy is available online at www.ReaderService.com or upon request from the Reader Service.

We make a portion of our mailing list available to reputable third parties that offer products we believe may interest you. If you prefer that we not exchange your name with third parties, or if you wish to clarify or modify your communication preferences, please visit us at www.ReaderService.com/consumerschoice or write to us at Reader Service Preference Service, P.O. Box 9062, Buffalo, NY 14240-9062. Include your complete name and address.

HII5

He looked up, hoping to see Natalie at the surface, thirty feet above. She wasn't there. His heart racing, Duff hurried through the rocks. Where the hell was she?

Movement ahead made him kick harder. As he neared a large boulder, he saw fins kicking and flailing. The smooth, pale legs attached could be none other than Natalie's.

When he was close enough he could see that a man had hold of her around the neck and was feeding her a regulator. He had her arms wrapped in what appeared to be weight belts, her wrists secured behind her.

Anger spiked, sending a surge of adrenaline through Duff. He raced for the attacker, holding his knife in front of him. He'd kill the bastard if he hurt one hair on Natalie's head.

Natalie's attacker must have seen Duff. He shoved Natalie toward him and kicked away from them.

HIEXP0216R

Duff grabbed her from behind and held her against him. She fought, twisting her body in a frantic attempt to get free.

Finally, Duff spun her to face him, pulled the regulator from his mouth and shoved it toward hers.

She stopped struggling and opened her mouth, accepted the regulator, blew out the water and sucked in a deep breath.

Duff turned her, slipped his knife between her wrists and sliced through the heavy weaving of the weight belt material, taking several passes before he freed her hands.

When she was free, she grabbed hold of his BCD and anchored herself with him. Natalie took another deep breath and handed the regulator to him.

They buddy-breathed for a couple more minutes until she was once again calm.

A shadow floated over them, indicating the location of the boat. One by one, they surfaced and waited their turn to climb aboard the boat.

Duff surfaced a second before Natalie.

When she came up, she spit her regulator out of her mouth and gulped in fresh air. She glared across at him. "Why the hell did you do that?"

He frowned. "What do you mean? I saved your life."

"I wasn't dying."

Turn your love of reading into
rewards you'll love with
Harlequin My Rewards

**Join for FREE today at
www.HarlequinMyRewards.com**

Earn **FREE BOOKS** of your choice.

Experience **EXCLUSIVE OFFERS** and contests.

Enjoy **BOOK RECOMMENDATIONS**
selected just for you.

PLUS! Sign up now
and get **500** points
right away!

Earn
FREE
REWARDS
HarlequinMyRewards.com
Join
Today!

MYR16R

THE WORLD IS BETTER WITH

Romance

Harlequin has everything from contemporary, passionate and heartwarming to suspenseful and inspirational stories.

Whatever your mood,
we have a romance just for you!

Connect with us to find your next great read, special offers and more.

 /HarlequinBooks

@HarlequinBooks

www.HarlequinBlog.com

www.Harlequin.com/Newsletters